# DEXTER CHASE

# The ACADEMY

Hardcore Submission & Domination Erotica

# WARNING

This book contains sexually explicit scenes and adult language. It may be considered offensive to some readers. This book is for sale to adults ONLY.

Please store your files wisely where they cannot be accessed by underage readers.

**About the Publisher**

**4Fun Publishing,** a member of **BLVNP Incorporated**, 340 S. Lemon #6200, Walnut CA 91789, info@blvnp.com / legal@blvnp.com

NOTE: Due to the highly emotional reaction of some people to works of erotic fiction, any email sent to the above address that contains foul language or religious references is automatically deleted by our anti-spam software and will not be seen. All other communications are welcome.

**DISCLAIMER**

Please don't be stupid and kill yourself. This book is a work of FICTION. Do not try any new sexual practice that you find in this book. It is fiction and not to be confused with reality. Neither the author nor the publisher or its associates assume any responsibility for any loss, injury, death or legal consequences resulting from acting on the contents in this book. Every character in this book is over 18 years of age. The author's opinions are not to be construed as the opinions of the publisher. The material in this book is for entertainment purposes ONLY. Enjoy.

# The Academy
## Hardcore Submission & Domination Erotica

By: Dexter Chase

ISBN: 978-1-68030-500-5

# Chapter 1

"Chris, what do you make of this?"

Chris looked over Mike's shoulder and read the advert that took up half the page in the educator's magazine he was reading.

"You keep saying you're fed up with the mediaeval way this place is run. How about applying to this new academy. The governing board is made up of the kids that are registered there. Can you imagine a bunch of eighteen year olds setting the standards for education and discipline?"

Chris finished reading the advert and then grinned at his friend and colleague.

"Never mind the standards; what about the salary?"

Mike had missed that. He was so amused by the remainder of the advert.

"Crikey, that is almost double our present pay scale. How the hell can they do that?"

Chris had read to the bottom and noted where the funding was coming from.

"That's easy—look at the source of funding. Remember about a year ago Donald Rush III; he died and left his billions to his teenage son. The boy is funding this school. I'm going to send for the prospectus and see what's in the detail."

A few days later these two young teachers sat down to read the detail.

The students were all specially selected as having potential that their old schools hadn't exploited. In other words, they were all bright kids. Most had lost time because they were bored with the teaching standards or were being diverted from study by personal and family problems, so most of them were already eighteen without having their high school graduation certificates. This academy was preparing them for college, and not just any colleges—the aim was to get them such high grades that places like Harvard and MIT would take them. Further details explained that each class had a leader who was a member of the ruling body and whose word was law in the classroom. Teacher qualifications were the highest any school would demand; many of the staff apparently had doctorates, and the contracts were for an initial one year. Penalty for breach of contract was severe.

"I'm going to apply Mike. It looks as though I'll be able to save 90% of my salary. Accommodation is on the school grounds and all food is supplied as well, at no charge. I won't even need to run a car. I know we only have bachelor degrees, but what the hell; nothing ventured, nothing gained."

Mike looked at it all again and thought he would join his old college buddy. Both of these men were 24 years old with two years teaching experience. They had first class degrees from a good college and their results in their present school were impressive. The academy was in Virginia, so both expected to be able to wear minimum clothes most of the year—expecting to be able to teach in light trousers and summer shirts.

Applications submitted and they were called for interviews. The instructions were very specific about dress code: fitted dress shirts and trousers, but the shirts should be short sleeved. Both men had gym fit bodies and looked impressive when they arrived together for their interviews. Chris was called first and was amused at the makeup of the interview board.

"Good morning, Chris. My name is Adam Chance and I'm the chairman of the governing body. Please make yourself comfortable."

Chris thought this was a fun way to start his new life if it happened. The whole board was made up of teenagers, or virtually teenagers. He settled down and studied the five boys sat in front of him with notepads on their laps. No table to divide them so he could scope them out. They were all wearing fitted shorts and T-shirts. They looked as sexy as all get out, giving Chris a tingle in his groin. Now it was time to impress, he guessed, so he replied to the greeting.

"Good morning gentlemen, thank you for calling me for interview."

Adam smiled at Chris and explained what the interview was all about.

"First name terms are standard throughout the school, Chris, with the exception of the class leaders and myself who will all be called 'Sir.' This board is made up of class leaders so you will know most of the 'Sir's' before you start."

Not an issue for Chris. Remembering these five hotties would be no problem at all.

"We are impressed with your CV and just wanted to have a look at you to see if you would fit in with the ethos of this school. We are all dedicated students, but have little time for the traditional methods of teaching or old-school type discipline. We have what you would term 'reverse methods' here. It is teachers that are punished here if the class considers they are underperforming. The likelihood of a student underperforming isn't even considered in the school rules. How do you feel about that?"

If Chris had asked what form of teacher punishment took, he would probably have run a mile to get away from here, but his overriding thought was that he would never be interrupted by bad behaviour in the classroom. That was almost the Holy Grail for a teacher.

"I have no problem with that at all, Sir. A class full of dedicated students will be delightful, allowing me to do what I find difficult in state schools—that is, teach."

"Yes, well that is why you are here. Your record in just two years is impressive and will no doubt be even better with our students. We note that you are also a registered soccer referee and we will be delighted if you will consider that as part of your duties. I'm sure our coach will be more than happy to integrate you into the sports side of this academy."

For Chris this kept getting better. He would be able to use locker and shower room facilities—without anyone realising he was gay. He would be there as of right.

"I would like that, Sir. I have always believed in the tenet, 'a healthy body houses a healthy mind.'"

Adam smiled broadly, looked at each of his other board members who all gave him the nod.

"We know your present salary, Chris, and would like to offer you a position, starting at the beginning of the next semester. The salary will be double your present one, and you will be inducted into the bonus scheme we run that is based on the exam results of your students, plus their personal assessment of you and your teaching methods."

Adam laughed then and continued.

"You will, therefore have every incentive to please your students. They will decide your bonuses, or not; and your punishment, if you ever need it."

Chris was over the moon with that. He still had some student loans to repay, but on his new salary he would pay them off and save money even if he only lasted one year here.

"Thank you, gentlemen, I will be most pleased to accept your offer."

"Very good, Chris. Your contract will be given to you as you leave this room. Please read and sign it before you go, and we look forward to seeing you on the 25th of August for your day of induction. You will commence lessons one week later, giving you that week to prepare your first lesson plans."

Chris could have danced out of that room but maintained his cool.

Adam was grinning like an idiot as he addressed his co-board members.

"So who is going to take his cherry if it hasn't already been taken?"

"I think that is my right, Adam. I am the history major and he is my teacher."

"Very well, Dominic. That will be posted in the Daily News. I think you are very lucky. He looks very well put together, and if I might say so, very sexy."

The posting was easy. 'Chris, the new history teacher will be Dominic's challenge.'

The post that would follow that would release Chris to the general school population.

Mike had a similar interview and was also accepted. Chris was gay and, after the initial embarrassments, would be a happy bunny with all these gorgeous teens. Mike would struggle as a straight boy, but the money and the penalties for breach of contract would keep him in the job for the year. After signing their contracts they were shown round the school and their accommodation. The one bedroom apartments were breathtakingly luxurious, with a fine restaurant on the ground floor.

"You can cook in your apartments, of course, but the restaurant is open to all staff and there is no charge to eat there, but only for lunch and dinner."

The trip back to their old school was full of happy talk.

"I won't believe it can possibly be this good until I am installed and experience it for real. Disappointing that I have to supply my own breakfast."

Then Chris dissolved in laughter.

The summer was a busy one for both young men. They had to close up their old apartments, pack their personal stuff and have it shipped to the new location. Chris kept his car thinking he could sell it when he was settled in at 'New World Academy' if he had no use for it.

~~~~

Chris was met by Dominic Ausberg.

"Welcome to the Academy, Chris. I am Dominic Ausberg and your class leader in the seniors."

"Thank you, Dominic. Oops, sorry, it may take a little getting used to, calling my students, Sir."

"Yes, well, I hope it won't happen too often. We are quite strict here and punishing staff is always embarrassing for them."

Chris was a little taken aback by that comment. What on earth did he mean *embarrassing*?

That thought disappeared when he was shown his apartment. It was even better than the one he and Mike were shown at their interview. The bedroom was where the major difference was. A queen-size bed and more open space. The kitchen was bigger as well with more equipment.

"I organised an upgrade for you, Chris, because I intend to spoil you if you make the grade. The larger bedroom and kitchen is to make it easier for you to have a guest to feed and sleep over if you wish."

Chris liked that idea, but who would he have to sleep over? Surely not students. That thought was cleared up quickly.

"I have no idea of your sexuality Chris, but all students are over eighteen so there is no restriction on your liaisons with them; and if you have a girlfriend, the odd night sleep over is not frowned upon, you just can't have guests in the staff restaurant. I can't afford to settle for anything under a 4.0 GPA, hence the upgrade. I believe in punishment and reward. This is part of your reward if I am a happy bunny, and let's hope you never have to see punishment."

There it was again.

"So, give me an idea of staff punishment."

"I don't think so, just work on the principal that you are going to be a model teacher."

He was shown round the campus including the student dorms. They were very pleasant but not private like his apartment. Classrooms were light and airy, state of the art and generally a place where one could study happily. They finished at the staff restaurant. On the wall by the entrance were a set of mail boxes.

"All your mail will go into your box and internal mail as well. Your syllabus and teaching notes are in History 1, which is your dedicated classroom. A school map should be in your mail box and the key is on your apartment key ring. Wander to your heart's content today, Chris, and settle in to prepare your lessons starting tomorrow."

"Thank you, Sir," was all Chris could think of to say.

He went back to his apartment where his luggage had appeared and spent an hour personalising it and unpacking. He wandered across to the academic block after that and settled into his classroom, familiarising himself with everything there. He loved all the projection equipment and realised he would be able to download pictures and notes from his laptop and project them onto the large screen behind his desk. Much more modern than his old school. Building his lesson plans was going to be a delight, and seriously professional. He moved his desk to the side of the dais more and angled it so that he could sit there and see both the screen and his students. Back to the staff block and into lunch, Mike was there, and they discussed their first impressions.

"Adam Chance is not only the head honcho, Chris, he is also my class leader. His induction was very professional. He finished it with a weird request. 'I have a rogue's gallery of all the staff, Mike. After lunch, say 1400 hours, will you bring Chris to the garden, outside the restaurant for me to take your photos? Don't worry about dress, you won't need any.' Those were his exact words. Don't ask me what that is all about."

Chris shrugged.

"Dominic was equally as weird talking about staff punishment. I think I'm going to read my contract very carefully after the picture show to see if I have missed something."

The garden was beautiful and would be a wonderful place to sit and relax after school finishes some days and at weekends. Adam showed up with a very professional looking camera and was dressed in just a pair of shorts, patently no underwear. His groin looked impressive, but both teachers noted that his body didn't compare to theirs—and he looked older than either of them. Discussed later, they decided he probably was older than them.

"My rogue's gallery is all nude so will you both undress for me."

Mike was first to reply.

"You are kidding, Sir, aren't you. That is quite out of order, if you were serious."

"I was serious, Mike, and if you read your contract you will know that the ruling board has pretty well total power over staff, so please just take your clothes off. Neither of you look as though you have anything to be ashamed of."

Reluctantly, both complied with the order. Adam had a broad smile on his face when he saw the result—both men were sporting gorgeous and quite large penises. They were flaccid and Adam thought that erect they would be incredibly sexy.

"Move close together so that you are angled, with your hips and heads touching but looking at the camera."

The resulting picture was quite stunning. Adam showed it to his two new teachers and Chris started to bone up. He hadn't realised how sexy Mike was. He was gorgeous with an incredibly sexy groin. The cock was about six inches long and quite thick.

*'Christ, if he is a grower I will be gagging to get that in my butt,'* was Chris's thought.

Adam noticed Chris chubbing up and told them both to dress again.

*'Dominic might have struck gold. I think his new teacher is gay,'* was his thought.

Mike joined Chris in his apartment afterwards, and they both read their contracts thoroughly.

"The lawyer that drew up this contract was one crafty bastard. Reading the terminology carefully it looks as though any student can recommend punishment of a teacher and the class leaders are allowed to specify the punishment. There don't appear to be any limits. We'll need to be super good Mike, or I can see embarrassing times ahead for us."

Mike was very unhappy with this turn of events. He was generally a very private person. Despite their long friendship, Chris had never seen him naked—until today. He worked out but never showered with his workout buddies. He didn't know it, but that was going to change quite spectacularly very soon.

By the end of their preparation week both young men were comfortable with their surroundings. They were, of course, a little apprehensive at the unusual set up here, particularly with regard to staff punishment.

# Chapter 2

Chris watched his first class file into the room. Nearly all of them looked as old, or even older than him, and he realised Mike looked younger than all of them.

"Good morning gentlemen. I hope you all had a great summer and are ready to work hard for the next thirteen weeks. I assume that with the familiarity you all showed in selecting seats that there are no new boys here. I would like you all to keep the same seats until I am familiar with you, and if we start at the back of the class on my left would you, in turn, stand up give me your name and your age."

Job done and Chris was surprised the youngest class student was Dominic Ausberg, his class leader. He was just eighteen.

Looking at Dominic he remembered he had to call him, Sir.

"Excuse me, Sir. Can I assume that, with the exception of yourself, I can call the rest of the class by their first names?"

"Yes Chris, that's fine. Now would you like to introduce yourself to the class with a potted history?"

Chris blushed. Faux pas on his part, he thought. He should have done that first.

"Yes of course. My name is Chris Lovell and I'm 24 years old. I have a bachelors in History from Harvard. I got there on a sport scholarship for Soccer. Wasn't really good enough so qualified as a referee instead. I did a B.Ed. as well and have taught for 2 years with above average success with my students exams. I know from my conversation with your board chairman that I should be able to improve my results here because you are all dedicated students. I am a bachelor, dedicated to my profession, so I will be available for private tuition or counselling outside of school hours for any of you that would like my assistance."

The boys all applauded and then allowed Chris to teach. At the end of the lesson he got his first jolt of subservience to his class leader.

"Chris, I understand that you have been appraised of the power that class leaders have."

Chris nodded, wondering what was coming.

"Good, because we have always enjoyed appraising our teachers from a physical side as well as their academic ability. Also, this lets them fully realise their position in the pecking order in this academy. So, will you kindly strip naked for us."

Chris started to bluster until Dominic cut him short.

"You will receive your first punishment after you are naked. Please don't make matters worse by any more protests."

Chris thought he would do as he was told and then talk to Adam about this. He stripped, blushing furiously. Standing naked in front of the class, he was further embarrassed when Dominic told him to stand still while he was fondled and brought to an erect state.

"Very nice, Chris. I'm sure you are going to be a very popular after-hours teacher. Now bend over your desk, spread your legs and again, don't move until you are told to."

Chris was aghast as he received ten slaps on his arse. They weren't particularly hard but the humiliation was monumental. Punishment complete and he was told to stand and dress.

Class dismissed and Chris went immediately to seek out Adam. No joy with that meeting.

"You have read your contract Chris. You know that class leaders have almost infinite power here. You will not be spanked or embarrassed again unless you truly deserve it because we realise that you hold the key to our success, or failure, so we don't want to alienate you."

Chris was very careful with his next class. He had not seen the class leader before but was almost drooling over this one. The boy was gorgeous. Justin Pierce was every gay man's wet dream. He stood to introduce himself to Chris. They were the same age.

"I managed to screw up 6 years of my life, Chris. You are going to make sure that I don't screw up any more by keeping me a 4.0 GPA. Any teacher that fails in that endeavour can expect plenty of grief from me."

Chris wanted to please this man, not because of the threats, but because he was drop dead gorgeous (DDG). If his character matched his looks he would make a wonderful lover.

Chris smiled as he replied.

"I am going to endeavour to keep all of you at least 4s, but you have given me even more incentive to succeed. Can I suggest that you come to see me in my apartment tonight so that I can get a better idea of your needs?

Justin smiled and replied.

"I will be at your door at 8 o'clock. In the meantime, would you like to strip for us? Because as you know we all like to see our new teachers—completely."

Chris was determined to impress this class, but this man in particular. As discretely as he could he rubbed himself as he stripped so that his cock was chubbed up a little. Success, it looked pretty good when he removed his mini briefs. Justin smiled after looking at it and told Chris to dress again. His thinking was that he would see it fully erect tonight and play with it as well.

End of instruction and Chris thought he would go for a swim before dinner and his meeting with Justin. There was a small lake a walking distance from the school, so he went there thinking it would be more private than the school pool. Walking through the woods to the lake shore, the first thing he saw was Justin, standing in the water up to his knees looking at him. The trunks were just short of indecent, but the package looked quite small. Chris hoped he would be a grower as he wasn't a shower. The body, though, was just incredible, and Chris knew that he would worship it if he got the chance. *Perfect* was the only way to describe it; size, shape, and musculature, in every way what he would choose to look like if he could, despite having a quite awesome body of his own. He dropped his towel on the sand, quickly disrobed leaving himself in a set of Speedos before walking in to talk to this apparition.

"Good afternoon, Sir, what a pleasure to see nearly as much of you as you saw of me last lesson."

Chris was grinning and Justin surprised him.

"We can change that instantly. Remove my trunks."

Chris didn't even think about looking to see if there was anyone else around. He just moved in close, dropped Justin's trunks and stood back to look. The cock was quite small, but in all honesty, Chris couldn't have cared less. The whole body was mouth-wateringly gorgeous. Justin turned round to show the rear before facing Chris again.

"Now, tell me what you would like to do with it."

"Perhaps we should wait until you are in my apartment tonight when we can discuss anything you like."

"Very well, I'm going to have a swim, but I'll see you at 8."

Chris nodded and watched as Justin pulled his trunks up again and swam away. He looked down then and realised he was sporting a monumental hard on. *'I bet Justin saw that'*, was his thought.

At dinner Chris was surprised at Mike's disclosure about his day.

"I don't know if I'm going to handle this, Chris, even for the money and the luxury living. Adam made me strip again today in his class, stripped himself and then made me lick his cock and balls. He was patently disappointed that I didn't get an erection and told me he would need to take me to bed to make sure I functioned normally. I guess you would have been monumentally hard and loved it."

Chris laughed outright.

"Oh Mike, you have no idea. I think this is going to be a gay boy's dream job. It might be a little embarrassing sometimes but I can live with that."

Mike nodded his head.

"You may be able to but I'm not sure I can handle it. I'm not anti-gay as you know, but I'm not into gay sex."

"Chances are that after they realise you don't enjoy it they will leave you alone, so I wouldn't worry too much. Just go with the flow for a few weeks and see what develops. Make me drool by telling me what our illustrious leader looks like naked.

"Oh, you'll love it. He has a thick nine inches with a small ball sac. I guess his body is pretty good as well, just not as good as ours."

"I wonder who selected the class leaders. I have met three and they are all DDG. I could go to bed with any of them happily, particularly Justin Pierce. Have you met him yet?"

Mike shook his head.

"No, I have a very light teaching schedule and have only met Adam and Dominic so far."

"Well, Justin is way more gorgeous than either of them and they aren't exactly chopped liver."

Mike began to relax. Chris could always calm him down and joke about things.

"I guess I'll be okay unless it gets really heavy."

Chris patted his friend's shoulder as he stood to leave.

"Must go, I have a tutorial with the most gorgeous guy in the school."

Mike grinned and told him, "Behave yourself then."

Chris walked off thinking that behaving himself was the last thing on his mind.

Justin knocked on his door only a few minutes after he got back from dinner and he was dressed in shorts and a polo. He looked delicious, quite edible, as far as Chris was concerned.

"Come in, Sir, make yourself comfortable. Can I get you a drink?"

"Just water, Chris."

Sat opposite each other in the lounge, Chris had a notepad with him.

"This is very casual, Chris. Wouldn't your study be more appropriate?"

Chris was a little confused by that comment.

"I don't think so. This isn't a formal tutorial, it is just a get-to-know-you session and to find out what help I can be to you."

"Very well, it is quite simple. I have no problems with your subject and don't expect to have if you are good. If I have any minor queries I will ask them in class. If you fall short of expectations I expect I will need extra tuition, but you will probably do that with a sore butt because others will be disappointed as well. On the personal side, I hope we can become friends. Of course, that won't happen if you are a straight guy because part of that friendship I'm looking for will be gay sex. I want to feel your lips round my cock at both ends."

Trying not to pant, Chris asked a question.

"I see. Can I expect any reciprocity on this or am I just to be a receptacle for your sperm?"

Justin had a broad smile as he answered that one.

"Oh there will be loads of reciprocity. I am a complete cock slut."

"In that case, Friend, would you like to come through to my consulting room for us to find out whether you like my ideas on reciprocity?"

Cocked eyebrow as Justin followed Chris. It soon returned to normal and was replaced with a grin when he saw the consulting room. It was Chris's bedroom.

"I suppose, as I am going to assess you, I had better let you take the lead this first time."

Chris could not have been happier as he moved in close to kiss Justin. He didn't think he had ever got an erection this quick in his life. The kiss was stupendous. Trying not to appear too eager, Chris started to undress Justin. It didn't take long. Polo, shorts, trainers. Job done and Chris sat back on his haunches and looked. Justin was erect with a cut cock hugging his belly, and Chris was pleased—the man was a grower. The little cock he had seen earlier was now about 7 inches long and has a respectable thickness. He moved back in to lick it and run his hands over the butt.

"You are even more gorgeous than when I saw you naked earlier. That cock is to be worshipped, and I promise to do just that if you will let me."

Justin looked down at Chris and stroked his hair.

"I have the feeling this will be mutual worship then, because I wanted to worship yours even without it being erect. Now how about standing up and letting me see the erect object."

No problem and Chris was standing naked while Justin fondled him and played with his ass, much the same as Chris' action had been.

"I top more often than bottom, Chris, but tonight I want you to make love to me. I am going to feel that monster creating havoc in my arse."

Chris helped him to his feet and planted another kiss on a beautiful pair of lips.

"Your wish is my command, with the greatest of pleasure."

Laid out on the bed with his legs spread, Justin looked so incredible that Chris nearly orgasmed just looking at him.

"You turn me on so much I am going to have to orgasm quickly and I'm going to be a waste of space, so, let's 69 and bring each other to orgasm so that I can make proper love to you."

Justin loved it. Chris was a consummate lover playing in all the right areas to make him gasp with the sensuality of the touching. Chris's mouth appeared to be everywhere at once on his cock and balls and the sensitive area behind the balls. His work on the glans and the frenulum had Justin wriggling all over the bed until both of them orgasmed with incredible force. Chris sucked Justin dry and then swivelled round to continue kissing and caressing this wonderful man.

"If you fuck me as sensuously as you blow me I think I will lock you away for my personal and exclusive use."

Chris looked into the eyes of this amazing creature.

"I don't think you will hear any dissent if you do. I think you are the most incredible human being I have ever seen in my life, Justin. I'll be your slave forever even if I do no more than what we have done already."

"Well, you had better do the next bit then to make sure I'm not going to disappoint you."

Chris didn't want Justin to touch him again because it would mean another early orgasm, so he slid between Justin's legs and used his hands to excite the anal area while his mouth was working on the cock and balls again. He slicked up his fingers to facilitate the finger-fucking. Justin was so turned on he helped the situation, pulling his legs back and wider so that it opened up his anus more, allowing Chris to rim him as well as finger him. The feelings rushing round his body had never been this strong with another lover, making him almost scream at Chris.

"For God's sake, Chris, fuck me, fuck me hard right now."

Chris positioned and with a well-lubed cock slid over a fully-relaxed sphincter and continued to full penetration with nothing more than a sigh of contentment from Justin. Nine rock-hard inches then carried out a clinically perfect fuck, slow and long, long and fast, hips rotating, hips still and just a straight fuck. Justin had never felt anything come close in the sensuality stakes, his almost continuous orgasms being testament to that thought.

The final orgasm for both of them was almost cataclysmic in its ferocity. Both men passed out. When Chris came to, he was lying over Justin's body, his cock still inside him. He eased his body weight off his mate but remained embedded in him. He moved it slightly and realised he was coming back to hardness. Slow humping soon had him as hard as a rock again.

"Do it, Lover. Fuck me hard and fast. I want more of your love juice inside me."

Chris obliged very quickly despite how many orgasms he already had.

"Oh God, Jus, you are incredible. I have never had sex like this in my life."

"Ditto, you amazing man."

After his final orgasm, Chris rolled sideways and the two men calmed down together, not even touching each other.

"There is no exclusivity allowed in the school, Chris, but I am hoping you will invite me to spend every night with you."

Chris slid up onto one elbow so that he could look down on this man.

"Is that allowed?"

"Just about, provided I don't impede other students from enjoying your body the remainder of the time."

"In that case, please come here every night after dinner. I'll carry out tutorials before dinner."

"You will still have to call me, Sir, in class, but know that I am sure I will grow to love you and you can call me anything you like in here."

Chris fell back onto the bed again, wondering how he could have found such an exquisite lover so quickly.

"Stay the night tonight, Justin."

"Oh yes, no problem."

# Chapter 3

The next day became crunch time for Mike. Dominic had heard from Justin how incredible Chris was as a lover. He also knew that Mike was straight and thought it would be fun to make Chris fuck his mate before he did the same thing. He thought he could do it with witnesses as well to embarrass the two teachers more. He had both of them for lessons the next morning and knew how he could get a punishment booked for both of them. In Chris' case he just said to him after the engineered incident, "Here at lunch time with a tube of lubricant." With Mike it was, "Chris's room at lunch time. I might as well punish you both together."

In Chris's lecture room at lunch time were all the class leaders, and Chris and Mike.

Chris and Mike were stood side by side at the front of the class with Dominic standing at the side.

"I thought, as it was two punishments of our new teachers, my fellow class leaders might like to watch. Both of you undress completely."

Quite used to this now, even Mike carried out the disrobing without any problem.

"Now face each other and play until you are both erect."

Mike's expression showed how much he disliked playing with Chris, but he did it and pleased the leaders by sporting a fantastic cock. Mike's was a quite thick ten incher, on his softly-muscled body it looked superb, and it made Chris' cock as hard as he had ever been.

"You may place your friend over your desk, Chris. Open up his anus and then fuck him. When you cum I will replace you, so you had better both undress me first and get me erect."

Mike looked as though he was going to die. He helped Chris get Dominic hard and gulped. He was looking at two serious pieces of man meat that were going to be planted in his ass very soon. Could he let it happen? Chris was reading his mind, because as he positioned him over the desk he whispered to him.

"I'll open you up carefully and I promise you that if you relax I will make sure I connect with your G-spot and you will have incredible feelings racing round your body."

Mike had a beautiful rounded butt keeping Chris very hard. He stroked it for ages, worrying the anus as he slid a finger down the crack. He slid one hand through his legs occasionally to play with the cock and balls. All the time whispering reassuring words to him. He opened Mike up very gently but could feel the tension in his body.

"You must try to relax Mike or this is going to hurt you so much."

When he thought the time was right, he lubed them both, placed his cock head at Mike's anal entry and told him to relax. Pushing gently, he managed to slide over the sphincter. At that point all the leaders got up and moved round to get the best view. Mike was devastated. Chris couldn't care less about the audience, he was fucking his best friend and it felt amazing.

Fucking very slowly, Chris leant in and spoke to Mike.

"You should be a gay man. You are a sensational fuck. I've always loved you, best friend, but this ratchets it up to another plain, you are a marvel."

Mike did relax more and became aware that Chris was right. His prostate was taking so much punishment that he came erect again and even managed an orgasm before Chris powered in for his own. Dominic followed, making Mike's eyes shoot open in surprise as ten inches buried itself in his ass. It felt incredible.

Dominic fucked Mike slowly, revelling in the feel of this cute teacher. Mike wanted to feel disgusted, but the assault on his prostate was so constant and exciting, his cock had never been harder and was producing pre-cum like never before. Dominic kept fucking until Mike complained he was getting sore, and then a few very fast and hard thrusts brought him to orgasm and he pumped Mike full. The leaders applauded and then all exited leaving Chris to look after Mike.

Mike looked wasted as Chris started to clean him up.

"Oh my God, Chris, that was incredible. That huge cock sliding in and out sent me into deep space. What the fuck have we got in our butts that give so much pleasure and pain?"

Chris laughed. He was so pleased his friend hadn't been traumatised by the sex.

"Just inside your anus is a gland called the prostate, lots of us call it our G-spot. As far as I'm concerned it's the centre of my sexual arousal. A few inches further in is the entrance to your large intestine, and entering that is like the initial penetration over your sphincter. Someone like Dominic enters it every time, and if he is good, you should get the pleasure feeling as he goes over your prostate and the pain as he enters your intestine, and the result is the most amazing orgasms, as you've just found out."

"I'm not gay, Chris, but I think I could put up with some more of that."

Looking very serious—well, trying to—Chris replied.

"I would be delighted to oblige anytime you like."

Mike got very serious then as well.

"Would you? Anytime I feel horny?"

Grinning like an idiot, Chris gasped out.

"Bloody hell, would I ever. I've always thought you were as sexy as all get out, and seeing you naked for our photo with Adam I almost disgraced myself."

That was case closed. Mike knew he could get a good fuck without having to give blowjobs and he wouldn't need to fuck Chris either. He thought that was disgusting. Unfortunately, Dominic had other ideas—he was seriously attracted to Mike, particularly the gorgeous cock which he wanted inside him at both ends at some time, as well as fucking Mike's gorgeous butt. It looked likely that Mike would be experiencing the full range of gay sex. Fucked by Chris and Dominic at least, receiving blowjobs from both and that would be okay, but having to blow Dominic and fuck him would not please him. The leaders realised it first, but then the students did as well, and the more sadistic ones took advantage of it just to humiliate Mike. Chris, on the other hand was happy with any of it. Truth, he was a complete cock slut and being forced to have sex with a bevy of gorgeous young men was heaven for him.

End of their first year and Mike told Adam that he would not be renewing his contract.

"I'm sorry, Adam. I love the academy; being able to teach instead of referee wrangling students is what I came into this profession for. I could live with the luxury of my accommodation as well with no problem until I get married. Despite being straight, I can even put up with being fucked and blown. What I can't handle is giving blowjobs and having to fuck another male."

Adam was looking at the end-of-year results for Mike's classes. Despite his youth, relatively speaking, Mike's students had outperformed previous teachers in this subject. His bonus would be the highest of any teacher; because not only were his results great, his students voted him top as well.

"We don't want to lose you, Mike, so will you hold off on resigning until I have had a word with the other leaders?"

"Sure, I've not started looking for alternative appointments yet."

Adam convened an emergency meeting of all the leaders who would be coming back for another year before they disappeared for the summer. He laid out Mike's position and asked for suggestions.

"We would be crazy to let him go, Adam. We have enough teachers for sex without having to use him for the two things he won't do. I'm sure most of us would be happy to be able to fuck him and give his fuck stick workouts with our mouths."

That was Tim Greely, one of the quieter leaders.

Justin was one of the less demonstrative leaders as well, so when he did speak, everybody listened and thought about it.

"I agree with Tim. I can handle just being able to fuck him after I have blown him."

"I'm with Justin on that one," came from another leader.

"Alright let's vote to give Mike the variations on his contract that will negate his need to fuck or give blowjobs, as long as you realise we are setting a precedent."

"A precedent for a first-class teacher is okay in my book."

That was it—a unanimous vote for Mike to stay on his terms. Adam sent for him after a new contract had been drawn up.

"Mike, we want you to stay. Here is a new contract, have a read of it and if it is satisfactory, sign it and let me have it back. You will note it is a rolling contract this time, the same as Chris. You are both considered exceptional teachers and we want to keep you."

Mike took it away, read it and discussed it with Chris.

"I've got the same Mike, except there is no variation to my usage by students, thank heavens."

The grin made it clear to Mike that Chris intended to be a cock slut for the foreseeable future.

"Won't Justin be disappointed?"

Mike knew that Chris and Justin could almost be considered an item. Justin slept with Chris most nights, but other students used him for sex a lot.

"I don't think so, Mike. He knows he will be out of here next summer and I will be remaining now that I have a rolling contract. We will have to work something out because when he finishes college, we want to live together permanently."

"Wow. *That* serious, huh?"

Chris blushed a little as he replied.

"Yes, definitely. I love the guy like you wouldn't believe. I know I come across as completely promiscuous, and I am, but I would be monogamous with him if I could."

"But you still give me blowjobs and fuck me."

"Yes, and you would be the exception if Justin and I do live together one day because you are my best friend and that comes with benefits."

Mike could see that Chris was embarrassed by that admission, so he slid across the floor and did what he considered the gayest thing of all. He kissed Chris quite passionately on the lips.

"You won't be getting many of those, but that was to show you that I love you, Best Friend."

Mike was amazed to see tears appear in Chris's eyes.

"What?"

Almost in a whisper Chris replied.

"I love you too. If you were gay I'd never have sex with another guy."

Mike was shocked. He had no idea that Chris felt that kind of love for him.

They were both very quiet after that until Mike stood up to go.

"I won't make things worse for you, Chris. I'll go to Dominic when I want fucking."

"Please don't. I love you so much, satisfying you gives me enormous pleasure."

Mike nodded, and left straight to Adam to agree his new contract, but he didn't give it to him at that time. Maybe he had a premonition.

With just one week to go to the end of the semester the graduating class had a party. All of the teachers were briefed that they would be used to the maximum at the party. For Chris and Mike, it was the first time that they had seen any of their colleagues naked. Every one of them was young and, to a man, gorgeous. It was apparent which ones were gay, which interested Chris. Staff turnover had to be quite high to keep the faculty average age so low. He thought the oldest teacher was only about 30 years old and he had a gorgeous body; obviously he worked out.

The party started in the gymnasium. Adam was, of course, the master of ceremonies and started by addressing all of the teachers.

"For some of you this will be a first. We will be stretching the terms of your contracts today, but the advantage for you is that you will be able to take this as your swan song if you wish to leave after it."

The teachers that were in their second year or more made it clear to the new ones that they could expect mind bending humiliation and punishment, but those that took it and signed new contracts would all get an additional bonus. The word spread quickly that the man standing next to Adam was the young heir that controlled the purse strings, Duncan Rush IV. He was still only just twenty and another gorgeous young man, but apparently a bit kinky.

Adam continued.

"I would like all teachers to return to their apartments and change into G-strings, or Tanga's, mustering here again and reporting to me. For the remainder of today you will act as servants for the graduating class and make your bodies available for whatever they wish."

Chris could understand why they were going to use the gym. All the equipment would allow loads of interesting apparatus to make the teachers display their wares. The examination table from the infirmary had been brought in as well and Chris noted that stirrups had been fitted. *'Why was that piece of equipment so popular in any kinky sex orgy?'* Chris thought looking at it. It certainly featured high on Chris's list of turn-ons in orgy films he had seen.

Chris found it difficult to remain flaccid looking at all the flesh displayed by his colleagues when they all reassembled. His aside to Mike was, "Can I come back as a student next semester. I think I could fuck every one of my colleagues, no trouble."

Mike sniggered, "You slut."

Adam took the stand again and spoke to the staff.

"Gentlemen, we don't expect you to be superb waiters but you will be judged on your standard of service today, so be careful how you serve drinks and food. If a student feels it is sloppy or poor service in any way, he will be rendering punishment, meaning some of you are likely to finish the day with sore butts, and not only on the outside. Your attire is a privilege that, once removed, will let us all know you have performed badly, making your future service more closely assessed."

"We could be okay, Mike, all the time we spent as barmen and waiters as we worked our way through college should be useful."

There was a 'dispense' bar set up, but no barmen. Any drinks ordered from a teacher had to be set up and served by the teacher.

There weren't many black students but Chris and Mike had both noted one particular one because he was so good looking. Chris, being a cock slut, had often wondered if he measured up to people's perception of his race. Now he was going to find out because the first teacher to fall foul of a student was one of the older ones. The drink served was unsatisfactory as far as Landon was concerned and, with no finesse, the guy tore the G-string off the teacher, laid him on his back, lifted and spread his legs, and with just a spit-slicked cock drove it into the guy's anus.

Chris and Mike managed to get a viewing position at the teacher's head looking down the body. It looked fantastic. Todd's legs were spread so that the knees were wider than his shoulders, and pushed down so far that they were resting on the biceps. Landon looked amazing, and that showed with Chris getting a monumentally hard erection. The guy was quite hairy but the body was a classic. Wide shoulders, narrow hip, slim waist, abs and pecs to die for and a long slender cock. Chris guessed about 9 inches. The action looked amazing. Landon was obviously fucking for enjoyment because Todd had a very respectable hard-on as well. After a few minutes Chris moved round and took a look at the rear view.

Chris nearly came on the spot when he saw it. Landon had told Todd to pull his cheeks further apart and the view Chris took in was of a well spread anus with a gorgeous black cock pistoning into it. When Landon came, Todd did as well. That should have been it, two happy bunnies wallowing in the afterglow of successful orgasms, but Landon was feeling wicked. With Todd still in the same position, Landon spanked him barehanded. That was too much for Chris, and he orgasmed as well without touching himself. Dominic saw it and acted on the sight. He pulled Chris out of the crowd of students and teachers that had watched Landon perform and made him stand on a weight bench. The huge wet patch in the pouch of his G-string was testament to his orgasm; it soaked almost all of it.

"Take your G-string off, Chris, show everyone your yucky groin and then suck the string clean of your cum. Mike, you can lick up the residue of cum on his body."

Mike put his hands across his chest, stood tall and square.

"Not going to happen, that is disgusting." Then he turned to Adam. "I think you had better forget our new contract. There are limits, even if they aren't specifically covered in the new contract, which perhaps they should be now."

Adam told Dominic that Mike was excused, but would accept as many cocks in his ass as Dominic considered appropriate.

The equipment table looked just right for Dominic's needs.

"Chris, prostrate yourself over the table, legs spread wide. Todd, secure his legs to the table legs. Mike, on your back at the other end. Swing your legs over and Chris, you grab the ankles and spread the legs as wide as you can bending them down so that his knees touch the bench at the side of his shoulders."

Two anuses were well displayed, and in Mike's case, cock and balls as well.

"Fuck fest now. No limits on personnel. Teachers can have a go as well."

Because Mike looked so sexy spread like a frog for dissection, he got the most attention. Chris was a great fuck, but Mike looked so sexy that several watchers creamed their underwear just watching, and plenty took advantage to have a fuck. Adam stopped it eventually because he thought they would be damaged if they were fucked too many times. Mike had never felt so humiliated in his life and was crying tears of shame, even though he had several orgasms. The power of the prostate was not to be denied. Chris loved it until he was sore, and then it became clear that the pain was overriding the sensuality.

They were dismissed and Chris took Mike back to his apartment and pampered him in a shower before creaming his anus very gently. He was so exhausted he fell asleep while Chris was doing it, so he covered Mike with a sheet, wrote a note to leave beside the bed and went back to his own apartment to clean himself up and think. The note just read, "Call me as soon as you read this. Chris."

Mike called just before dinner time and sounded okay, so Chris wandered across to his apartment. Mike had started packing his things.

"What are you doing Mike?"

"I'm packing to leave. I'm not prepared to accept that amount of abuse and humiliation. I know I accept being fucked, but that really is all I'm prepared to accept," grinning at his best friend he continued, "Plus as many blowjobs as anyone wants to give me."

"You can't leave, you've been my best bud for years and even if I found a soul mate I would still want you with me."

Chris sounded really upset, making Mike look very closely at his friend. What he saw was the love, and desperation.

"Tell me it as it is, Chris, without any bullshit."

Chris's shoulders slumped and he couldn't look at Mike. Tears started streaming down his face as he replied.

"If you were gay, I'd ask you to marry me and be with me forever. I'd swear never to have sex with another man and be your slave. I love you so much. I'll do anything for you. I would leave here as well to be with you except that I have already signed a new contract."

That all came out in a rush and then Chris fell to his knees and just sobbed. Mike was shocked. He had no idea that Chris felt like this. He dropped to his knees as well and pulled Chris into a cuddle. He didn't know what to say so he just stroked his friend until he calmed down, by which time he had found some words to say.

"Come on Buddy, let's go and eat. I need time to think about this. I love you as well Chris, but I've never thought of it as the kind of love that man and woman have for each other."

Chris looked into the eyes of the man he thought he would die without.

"I'm sorry Mike, I never meant to fall in love with you like this."

Going for a meal gave Mike time to think. The only answer to his thoughts was another meeting with Adam, so after their meal he told Chris he needed half an hour to run an errand and then he would see him in his apartment. He found Adam beavering away at work in the academy admin office.

Sat comfortably, Mike appraised this young administrator carefully.

"I don't think that what I'm asking for is a choice thing for you, Sir. If you don't agree, you will definitely lose me, and you will lose Chris, but in such a way that you won't be able to sue him for breach of contract. I don't feel I can tell you any more than that. What I am proposing is that you vary my contract again so that mass orgies, like today's party, are not part of my agenda. I am definitely a straight boy and have put up with a lot more than you would expect purely for the sake of Chris. I am prepared to be fucked, and sucked, mainly in private, but with no more than two or three students present. I won't fuck anyone and I won't give blowjobs. If a new class leader wishes me to strip and play with me, I can handle that in the class room; I'm not ashamed of my body or my manhood. If I'm unsatisfactory I'll accept punishment because I know that keeps me on my toes. I love the teaching environment in this academy, otherwise I wouldn't even consider it. You realise it is totally bizarre and wouldn't be believed by anyone who hasn't experienced it?"

Adam looked at Mike while he thought about it and then grinned.

"I think for full awareness of what I am considering I need to see you naked and erect again, so, while you are still under your old contract, strip for me."

Adam loved it. Looking at Mike, naked, really was amazing. His body was so beautifully put together without the gross musculature of the bodybuilder, but definitely a gym fit individual. He walked round his desk and gently played with Mike's cock and balls, bringing him to an erect state.

"Sit down Mike, I'm going to blow you to orgasm."

Definitely no argument from Mike. A blowjob was still the best way he knew to orgasm and Adam was an expert. His orgasm a few minutes later was fantastic and he voiced it to Adam.

"You aren't playing fair. That is, as always, incredible; even better than the orgasms I have from my prostate being attacked."

Adam grinned and replied.

"That is because I'm not straight and that cock is to die for."

Dressed again and facing Adam, Mike waited for the decision.

"This is really difficult for me because I have to be careful that by setting this precedent, I don't alienate other straight members of staff. Fortunately, the boss is still here so I can consult with him. I'll do so straight away if you would come back in an hour's time."

Mike had seen the boss at the orgy and had been impressed with the way he behaved. He was still only a boy really, not even graduated from college yet, but he carried himself well and looked impressive in his fitted shirt and shorts.

Mike went back to Chris's apartment and they sat talking about the upcoming holiday.

"Justin is coming home with me for part of the holiday, Mike. I want Mum and Dad to meet him as I am hoping he will be my lover long term. He knows I love you and I think that makes him even better as a lover because he tries harder. He knows that whatever happens I'll always be prepared to show you that my love for you is an enduring one."

Mike was surprised at that and realised that the only thing he could hope for was that Chris's love for Justin would grow and swamp this other love.

His cell phone rang just as he was about to leave for Adam's office again. He was instructed to bring Chris with him. When they arrived they were introduced to Duncan, and were told to call him by his first name.

"I have seen the stats for your first full year and I have to agree with Adam that we don't want to lose either of you. I don't like precedents; however, I am prepared to let this one go. I have briefed Adam on how it should be handled, and provided you keep silent on the matter, Mike, I'll agree to your terms. Your new contract is being drawn up as we speak."

Chris looked bewildered and Mike just touched his arm to gain his attention.

"I'll explain later."

"I want two things from you, Mike, before I go home, and now would appear to be the best time to take them. I want a photo of you with Chris and myself, all of us naked. Then I want a little orgy with you two and Adam where you, Mike, are on the receiving end of three cocks and you will get at least one blowjob."

Mike knew that this would get him another year with Chris at this academy—time, hopefully for Chris and Justin to be in a solid relationship.

"Okay, Chris, multiple fun for us."

Chris was bewildered, but if he was going to be able to fuck Mike and give him a blowjob he wouldn't complain. They retired to the bedroom in Duncan's guest suite where Adam immediately joined the others, naked.

"I will be the master for this, Mike and Chris. I say, you do, no hesitation."

They both agreed and the orgy commenced.

# Chapter 4

Mike's thought as he stood in front of this well-buffed and wealthy young man, who was patently another gay guy, was how well put together he was—nearly all the gays were. He was better than he would have been because of Chris. He had become quite astute at recognising the gay students and staff, as well as the pure thrill seekers. His guess was that many of them had underperformed as a result of pressure due to their sexuality. In the case of the teachers that remained for second years and more, it was quite obvious that they were gay as well. He guessed that over time the whole school would be gay.

But now, back to the present. Duncan told Mike to sit in a comfortable chair, and for Adam to do the same.

"I'm going to give Mike a blowjob first to see how exciting he is. And you, Chris, can do the same for Adam."

Mike noticed that Duncan was already as hard as an iron bar, and as he knelt in front of him he produced a tube of lubricant. For about ten minutes Duncan just caressed Mike's body paying little attention to his groin. Even Chris didn't spend that much time just stroking him and playing with his nipples. When Duncan did progress to the cock, Mike was already as hard as he ever got. The attack then on his cock and balls had him gasping. It was nearly all tongue work, just using his hands to move the cock away from his tummy to allow for sucking. With both hands spreading his piss slit, Duncan managed to just touch a little of the sensitive skin in Mark's urethra, making him gasp with the sensitivity of it. Then the tongue moved to the rim of the glans, worrying the frenulum the most, before licking his way down the shaft until he got to the balls, which he took straight into his mouth and swabbed for ages while he used his hands now to continue cock play. When he was panting with the eroticism of Duncan's attack, he was told to slide down the chair a little more. Duncan then started on his anus, licking up and down the crack before using his hands to spread the cheeks more to start tongue fucking him. It was obvious that Mike didn't need opening up so he returned to the cock and sucked him to an intense orgasm. When he was sure he had all of Mike's sperm he used the lube on Mike's ass, lubed his cock and then told Adam and Chris to hold Mike's legs up and wide. Still in the kneeling position he entered Mike smoothly in one go with no sign of pain. Duncan was so turned on he lasted only a few minutes before blasting Mike's insides with several very powerful jets of cum. Mike, as usual, was terribly embarrassed. Not because of Chris looking down at the cock pistoning in and out of his arse—but Adam, jacking himself and orgasmed about the same time as Duncan, spraying his seed all over Mike's face. There was no doubt though that sexually, Mike had enjoyed it, his orgasms being testament to that.

"My God, Adam. Why would anyone want to waste time being blown when they can have what I have just experienced? Why don't you fuck him now while Chris gets me ready to fuck him?"

Duncan went to clean up and came back into the bedroom in time to watch Adam sink his cock into Mike. He went to lay down on the bed and told Chris to get him hard again and then fuck himself on the hard cock. For Chris that was a delight. He thought Duncan was a very sexy man and found it easy to satisfy him.

The resulting orgasms all-round were very satisfying. Cleaned up and dressed, they all sat around in the lounge and Duncan spoke to all of them. He found out where Mike and Chris lived before making a suggestion.

"I would very much like to entertain you both at my home in Connecticut for a long weekend sometime during your vacation. I would get my private jet to pick you both up at your nearest airport and return you at the end of the weekend. Adam will be there as well, and a few other students. In your case Mike, you will not be required to join in any of the sexual romps, and Chris, you can join in as you will."

Details were worked out and the teachers left. In Mike's apartment they talked—or more precisely, Mike talked and Chris listened.

"I have negotiated a new contract that limits my exposure to gay sex to manageable proportions, so I'm remaining for another year."

Chris was in tears again. Tears of relief.

"I'm so pleased," was all he could get out before Mike had him in a serious cuddle.

"I wish I was gay, Chris. I will never have someone in my life that can thrill me sexually the way you do, but I wouldn't be any good for you.

I just don't think I could blow you or fuck you. We would both end up unhappy."

Chris thought that was true. He would just have to get over it. He had, after all, got Justin who was an amazing creature.

Mike went home to his parents. Chris did as well but he had Justin with him. They were going to split their summer: half with Chris's parents, provided the admission that Justin was his lover was received okay, and the other half with Justin's family who already knew he was gay. Mike would join them at different times for a week here and there.

Duncan didn't hang about. The boys had only been home a week when they got the call. Justin, Chris and Mike found themselves at a huge country estate with about a dozen students from the school. The house staff were all young and gorgeous, and the security detail was eye-wateringly sexy. Duncan was the consummate host, personally settling them into their rooms. He had put them into two double suites with a connecting door.

"I have no idea how you want to work your sleeping arrangements so this leaves you to sort it in private."

Chris wanted Justin to sample Mike so he glibly said, "Okay, I guess its three in a bed then."

Justin didn't mind, but Mike looked at Justin and winced. He was like Chris—he thought Justin was absolutely the most gorgeous human being he had ever met. Would sex with him be exceptional? And more importantly, when he saw Justin naked, would all his normal inhibitions and restrictions still apply? The body was incredible. The butt was such a beautiful shape he was sure that naked it would be breath-taking; and if the cock was as pretty as the rest of him would he be prepared to suck it and swallow his sperm?

Discretion being the best part of valour, Mike said nothing.

They joined the other guests for an early BBQ because it was Duncan's wish that they have an early romp. Chris and Justin were joking about which of the young guests they would like to fuck and which ones they wanted to give them blowjobs. Justin winked at Chris before stating quite clearly.

"I would like Mike to fuck me and give me a blow job to get me properly in the mood."

Mike heard and grimaced before stating quite clearly.

"Dream on. If you want cock in your arse, I suggest Chris. He is such an expert. And the same goes for the blowjob."

Lots of laughter then, but Duncan had heard and thought he would have a great opener for the orgy. So after the food had been cleared away he took everyone to a bedroom that opened onto the garden.

"I know that Jake thinks Mike is an incredibly hot guy and is looking forward to seeing him when he starts at the academy next semester. I thought it would be a great opener this evening for us to watch this young man fuck Mike."

Everyone applauded and Mike turned bright red. He realised he was going to be an exhibition fuck for a future student, and even though Duncan had told him joining in the orgy was voluntary, he felt he had to go along with it. Two of the houseboys, who were very cute, stripped Mike and played with him until he was rock hard. Jake then led him to the bed and made him get up on to it doggy fashion, legs well spread. With no preamble he lubed Mike and himself and slid into him. Mike turned to look. He was so surprised being taken this quickly. The feeling was good, but not as exciting as being fucked by Chris. He realised that if Chris was like Jake he would probably revert to total straight guy status. Jake fucked him for a few minutes, quite gently, then he called Scottie to join him.

"Why don't you lie on the bed, Scottie, and let Mike fuck himself on your man rammer."

Scottie lay back comfortably and Mike sat over him and slowly sank on to Scottie's cock. Mike realised that this boy was another gorgeous creature, and his cock was much more to his liking. It was substantial and hit his prostate almost every entry. He was enjoying it until Jake climbed onto the bed and told him to lean forward. He then felt another cock slide up to his anal entry and pressure being applied until it slid over his sphincter.

"Oh God, that hurts, please take it out."

Jake held on to Mike's shoulders to keep him impaled on the two cocks. There were gasps from the onlookers who were all moving round to get a good look.

"Relax, Mike, the pain will soon go."

He couldn't move, so he took deep breaths and tried to relax. Jake felt it and continued the penetration. The next half an hour was unbelievable. Scottie just stayed still because Jake sliding in and out was as stimulating as him doing the fucking. Scottie's long slender cock was in heaven. This was his first double fuck—but knowing Mike would be at school with him and Jake next semester—it wasn't going to be his last.

After about ten minutes they had Mike lay on top of Jake on his back and his legs were pulled back and wide. The view now as Scottie slid back in was amazing garnering gasps as everyone could see quite clearly both cocks stuffed well up inside Mike. This time it was Scottie doing all the work, but it was Jake who screamed out first that he was coming. His orgasm was quite violent almost making Scottie pull out. The sensation was so fantastic that Scottie started as well and Mike could hardly believe the feelings in his arse. He looked round at all the other guests, and felt so embarrassed as he realised that he had orgasmed several times and his tummy and chest were covered in his own cum. When the two boys slid out of Mike the applause was deafening.

"Well done teach, I'm going to have some of that next semester."

Mike looked daggers at the boy but it didn't make any difference as all the other students said the same thing.

That start to the orgy had everyone so turned on that it was quite late by the time the last of the guests headed for their rooms, having been reduced to firing blanks. Chris had pleasured and then fucked Duncan— he thought that was appropriate for initiating the fucking of Mike at the academy. Justin became a voyeur for the evening, refusing any advances from the other guests because he was going to have Chris make love to him that night. Chris knew and limited his actions so that he was still quite fresh for his lover.

Mike went to bed by himself, telling the others he was so beat he just wanted to sleep. Chris and Justin had their love in and all three looked fresh when they sat down to breakfast.

"That double fuck was amazing Mike. How does your arse feel this morning?"

Mike tried to look serious but it was difficult having realised how fantastic two cocks in his arse had been. *'Perhaps Chris and Justin will double fuck me as well, now that they know I can take it,'* was his wicked thought.

Mike realised after further thought that he had revelled in the sex last night. Jake was quite petite with a lovely little body and a very adequate cock, but Scottie was stunning with at least nine lovely inches of man meat. He thought he would quite like to suck that. The thought brought him to his senses when he realised these were proper gay thoughts. *'Oh my God, am I gay?'* That thought brought with it major complications to the lives of three guys: Mike himself, Chris and Justin. Mike needed to talk to someone about this, but the one person he would like to talk to, he couldn't—Chris.

Mike was so pleased that after the massive orgy of the first night that the remainder of the weekend settled down to a much civilised party with loads of activity, not all of it sexual. He allowed a couple of the new students that would be joining after the summer to fuck him, and on all three nights after that he had sex with Chris and Justin. This was the sex that he loved the most. Chris as always was so gentle and caring, and Justin followed his example. He loved it when Justin was fucking him and Chris was giving him a blowjob.

How could he not be gay!

Nothing was settled, and Mike was quite apprehensive when the new semester commenced.

It was Jake that caused him the most problems. The boy was quite petite, also quite shy. He had been bold at Duncan's orgy because of the encouragement he received, but in Mike's apartment, he was putty in Mike's hands. The lovemaking became quite intense and Mike ended up 69-ing with him. The first time he didn't take Jake's cum in his mouth, but he did later—and then the big one.

One night, the lovemaking had become so intense that Mike wanted to fuck Jake. The resulting orgasms had Jake crying with happiness.

"I love you Mike. I think I did, the first time I saw you. Please fuck me again. Feeling you inside me is the most incredible thing that has ever happened to me."

Mike did, and after Jake had left he sat and thought about the events of the evening. He realised he loved Chris, but only as a friend. Okay it was with benefits, but what he was beginning to feel for Jake was the kind of love that Chris had wanted for them. Was Jake the catalyst for Mike's revelation of his sexuality?

The crunch came for Mike when Chris realised that Jake was sleeping with Mike almost every night, the same as Justin was with him.

A free period when they could talk in the staff room and Chris brought up the subject.

"I know from conversations I hear in class that Jake is mainly passive, but he sleeps with you nearly every night. Am I missing something here?"

Mike looked like the deer caught in the car headlights.

"I'm sorry Chris. You know I love you but it has always been as a friend, okay, with benefits, but I have never felt a romantic love for you and I thought that was because I was a straight boy. Jake has changed that. I am beginning to love him so much, and being the top has come easily to me with him. Please try to understand. I still love you, and probably will as long as I live. I'll probably still enjoy sex with you as well, provided Justin and Jake don't mind."

Chris was struggling with this revelation. He realised he was being greedy. He wanted Justin and Mike.

"I know I'm crazy, Mike. I love Justin and thought I could have both of you. My mind isn't as simple on the subject as yours. I feel a romantic love for both of you and that's not very practical."

Grinning like an idiot now that he could see Chris wasn't too upset, he made a suggestion.

"Well, if Justin and Jake can feel the same way, perhaps we can have a four way marriage."

Chris giggled then. "Mmm, I could definitely handle that. Jake is really cute. Three gorgeous butts to fuck would probably be enough for me."

Mike breathed a sigh of relief. No trauma. Chris had found a romantic love that was reciprocated; he could now let go of his romantic love for Mike.

"I'll talk to Jake about us having a four-man love in. I'm sure it would be magical."

"I'll do the same with Justin. You realise that if we go this route, you and I are going to be seriously overworked on the sex front because there will still be the requirement to accede to student demands for sex."

"That won't worry you, will it?"

Chris grinned. "Not a bit."

Mike got serious then.

"Be careful, Chris. You could get hurt with Justin if you aren't. He is monogamous with you, isn't he?"

"Oh fuck, I never thought about that. He puts up with other students taking advantage of me because of my contract, and me with you because of our friendship, but yes, I guess he could get antsy if I widen the circle. I'll have to talk to him."

Life got even more complicated for the two friends. They walked into the gym a couple of nights after that conversation to find Jake secured to the wall by one wrist, naked. He was looking a little frightened.

Mike went over to him.

"What are you doing there, Lover?"

"It has come out that you fuck me and give me blowjobs. I'm sorry Mike. I didn't think about your contract and guys have picked up that we are close. I said what a wonderful lover you were and they know I'm passive, so two and two made five and I was found out. I now have to endure student punishment. For two hours every night for a week I am secured here by Adam and any student can punish me either with sex or a chastiser. There are no limits so they can be disgusting if they want to."

Mike could see that the strap was long enough for Jake to kneel so he could be fucked, made to suck and bent over to punish. He knew there was no appeal. Adam's word was law. At that moment Adam came into the gym as well.

"You don't get off scot free, Mike. You have allowed the exclusions on your contract to lapse without informing me, thereby denying students the access to your body that every other teacher has to permit. I will discuss your punishment with the other class leaders and inform you when we have made a decision. In the meantime, you will have no private sex with Jake. The only contact you may have with him for now is in public."

Mike was gutted. He sat down opposite Jake and watched the action, looking quite devastated.

The first student to take any action made Jake face the wall with his feet three feet away and wide spread, hands on the wall also wide spread. He then proceeded to give Jake ten with a leather strap, hard enough to elicit gasps from Jake as each one landed. Punishment finished and the boy made Jake turn and kneel. The boy received a blow job then and orgasmed over Jake's face.

"Do not touch my cum until you are released from the strap."

Mike remained in the gym for the two hours, not working out, just watching Jake. At the end of the two hours when Adam came in to release him, Mike took him to the shower room and pampered him. When he was calmed down, and his sore bottom creamed. Mike left for the staff quarters patently very upset. By the end of the week Jake was a mess. He looked hunted, had retreated into himself and avoided any contact with Mike. Mike's punishment by comparison was mild. He was to receive ten strokes of the strap every night for a week and accept at least ten boys cum down his throat.

Chris was so incensed he went to see Adam.

"Both of those sets of punishment were brutal and over the top. You have sunk in my estimation. You can be quite certain that neither Mike nor I will be renewing our contracts for another year."

Adam was pissed off with that and decided to talk to Duncan to see what he thought about making life bad for the two teachers for the remainder of the year. What he didn't know was that Chris would start a regimen of disinformation, meaning that none of his classes would get first class passes. He persuaded Mike to do the same. It would mean that none of the graduating class would get guaranteed places at top colleges. That would also punish the students that had been horrible to Mike and Jake during their punishment period, and that continued with Mike afterwards as well. The only upside to that was that Jake became more worried about Mike than feeling sorry for himself and the old relationship blossomed.

"If you and Chris give me extra tuition in your subjects and help me with the others, I might be able to graduate this year and leave at the same time as you and Chris."

Mike thought that would be great and Chris fell into the plan. Justin was a first class student so all four of them spent most of their free time tutoring and learning together.

Duncan wouldn't sanction any extra action on Mike because he didn't want to alienate the teacher. He had no idea that the action already had.

Because Chris' apartment was the biggest, they congregated there every night after dinner to study. Justin and Jake both knew what disinformation had been passed out in class and were given the correct information in the tutorials. End of term results still mirrored the expected.

It would be the final exams that would show how effective Chris and Mike's war had been. They felt a little guilty about the students that would fail, or get lower grades that had not been horrible to either Mike or Jake, but they would all still pass and go to college, just maybe not the best ones.

The closeness these four felt eventually showed with a sexual bent. One evening when they had finished the tutorial earlier than expected, Chris, outrageous as ever, made the suggestion.

"Our boys have been so good tonight, Mike. Do you think they deserve a reward?"

Mike guessed where this was leading and gave his okay.

"Alright, Justin and Jake. You can be as outrageous as you like for the next couple of hours and take a reward for being such excellent students."

The grin plastered across Chris' face was enough to get Jake and Justin in a huddle while Chris and Mike went to the kitchen to get drinks and check that the bedroom was set up, bed stripped to just a bottom sheet and pillows, lubrication on the bedside table.

"We have decided, as all of our troubles stemmed from Mike being late discovering his sexuality, that we are going to spit roast him first. Then we are going to do the same to Chris for being a cock hound. If we are satisfied that you have performed enthusiastically, we will finish with Chris fucking Jake and Mike fucking me. Any unsatisfactory action and you will be spanked with our bare hands with you across our knees."

Justin finished that little speech with a huge grin across his face. But that wasn't as wide as Chris's grin.

Chris was fascinated watching the action. Mike was on the bed on his back with J&J either side of him. They kissed him and pampered him getting him a very hard erection. They took turns sucking him as well, which soon had Mike spacing out; it was so erotic having two sets of hands and two tongues working on him. Before he could cum, they turned him over and had him doggy fashion. Jake straddled him and pulled his cheeks apart while Justin tongue- and finger-fucked him. His first orgasm made a mess on the towel that Justin had placed under him and then he entered Mike at the same time as Jake slid his cock into Mike's mouth. Chris had a no-touch orgasm as Justin powered in for his last strokes and Jake filled his mouth with his orgasm. Chris was pleased to see that Mike had cum again. All calmed down and J&J discussed it and decided that Mike had been pretty good, the understatement showing in the wide grins on their faces. The repeat performance with Chris was equally successful.

The final act was a humdinger. Jake was flat on the bed, legs spread and hooked behind Justin's arms. Justin was straddling Jake so that they could 69. Mike fucked Justin doggy fashion and Chris fucked Jake in the missionary position. Jake and Justin were able to play with each other as they blew each other as well, but they could also let their hands wander and both of them finger-fucked Chris and Mike as well. The four resulting orgasms were almost cataclysmic in their intensity. They fell in a tangled heap while they recovered, and individually they all thought it was the hottest sex they had ever taken part in.

Surprise, surprise—Jake and Justin decided that the sex had been second rate and therefore a spanking was on the cards. They looked serious as they had Mike and Chris over their knees. The spanking consisted of some serious finger-fucking and loads of erotic tingling slaps on their butts. They were stood in front of their partners after that with major erections which were quickly dispatched with blowjobs.

All showered and dressed afterwards, Justin summed up all of their thinking.

"That is the best sex I have ever had, but I am wasted, and if we do that very often I will definitely fail my exams, because I'll never be able to concentrate in class the next day."

They made a pact to only do it on a Saturday night, but in all honesty it was never quite as good as it had been the first time. The variation on action did make it a load of fun and bonded these four young men in a deep and abiding friendship.

Their love and respect for each other did mirror itself in the way Chris and Mike handled the students. They stopped the disinformation and took their revenge on the horrible students by marking down their course work. The overall result was what they wanted. The good guys passed with high scores and the shits with low scores. Mike and Chris took a few beatings in the class room, but nothing they couldn't handle.

The worst one was one of Chris's students who was very angry at the low mark Chris gave him for one paper.

"I'm not convinced that is a fair mark Mr. Lovell, and I am going to show you my displeasure at the end of this lesson. It is the last lesson of the day so I won't feel constrained by time, and I am inviting the remainder of the class to witness it. You know I can do this Justin, so I don't want any grief from you."

End of lesson and Mr. Nasty walked to the front of the class and found the long wooden pointer that Chris uses when he had projections on the large screen.

"Strip naked."

This was nothing new so Chris did finishing at display.

"Now play with yourself, but stop just before you cum."

Chris still found this very embarrassing and pleased his punisher by blushing.

The remainder of the class had stayed to watch this, and several were nursing hard cocks as they watched Chris with his lovely cock jacking off. Nearly there and he stopped.

"Now, lay over your desk, grip the front and spread your legs wide."

He was made to spread them wider and move his feet in close to the legs which had the effect of pushing his arse out. Mr. Nasty dropped his trousers and with minimal spit on his cock rammed it into Chris, all the way in one go. Chris was used to quite large penises reaming him out, but this one was very thick, and with little lubrication, was very painful. He grunted but that was all despite being viciously raped. He could feel the cum running down his leg after the student pulled out. What he didn't know was that it was mixed with blood. Mr. Nasty picked up the pointer again and delivered a searing blow to Chris's butt. The stroke was so powerful that the pointer shattered. Chris screamed with the pain and passed out. The skin wasn't broken, but it was nothing short of a miracle considering the power behind the stroke.

In the sick bay, the resident nurse attended to the splits in his anus and layered the bruised pointer stroke with cream before strapping it with layers of cream left to soak in overnight.

"He should be okay. Make him take two of these and put him to bed."

Chris was taken to his apartment face down on a stretcher and transferred to his bed. Justin didn't leave him until he got up to make breakfast. Out of stubbornness, Chris made it to class. When Mr. Nasty walked in, Chris told him to leave.

"I will not teach you for the remainder of this semester."

Adam got stroppy. But Chris wouldn't give in. There was nothing in the rule book to cover this, so it was left and the boy concerned home-schooled himself in History until the exam—which he failed.

# Chapter 5

Mike and Chris tendered their resignations after final exams. Duncan came to the academy to try persuading them to withdraw them. He had been given a heads-up on the papers by a contact at the examining board. His comment to Duncan had been unequivocal.

"The History and Finance papers from your academy look as though they will produce better results than you achieved last year, Duncan. Your teachers in those subject should make you extremely pleased."

For all his youth, Duncan had been serious in his aims when setting up the academy and wanted to keep Chris and Mike, hence the personal intervention in this instance. Adam would be leaving this time making it easier, he hoped, to make them change their mind.

Chris and Mike were summoned to Adam's office and were surprised to see Duncan there.

"Come in gentlemen, please sit down. Can we get you a drink? Let me suggest champagne even though it is only 10 o clock in the morning."

Mike and Chris looked at each other with a *what the fuck is this all about?* expression on their faces.

Settled with drinks, Duncan cut straight to the chase.

"I don't know the full story of why you have resigned. Would you first off fill me in on the details?"

Mike took him blow by blow through Jake's punishment. What he had not told Chris, and Jake had never told anyone, was the last student to punish him on his last day, and the same with Mike on his last day, had made them blow him and then had pissed in their mouths.

Duncan was shocked. That was disgusting and had not been catered for in the punishment regime.

"Jake was quite traumatised by it and it nearly ended our relationship. Wherever Jake goes to college I am going to try for an appointment to a high school close by."

"What about you, Chris?"

"I was just so disgusted with Adam's decision that I wanted to leave immediately. As it is I'm hoping to do the same with Justin as Mike is with Jake."

Duncan thought about this for a few minutes.

"Thank you both for being so frank. Could you leave this with me and join us again for lunch in my guest suite?"

No point in refusing so they agreed to the suggestion. Back at Chris's apartment, Chris spoke first.

"What do you think about that?"

"My guess is that Duncan doesn't want to lose us, but now that he has the facts, needs time to think what he can do."

What Duncan did was talk to the Dean of Admissions at Princeton. He convinced the dean that Jake and Justin would get their school certificates with exceptional grades, would be a credit to the university and would be fully funded by the Rush Family Trust. The Dean accepted that, already knowing Duncan who was a sophomore at the university.

At the lunch table in between courses, Duncan asked Mike what it would take to keep him at the school.

"Quite honestly Duncan, I can think of nothing. The punishment regime for staff is just too over the top. I'm not saying it should be stopped because it obviously works, but the abuse I have suffered is unacceptable, and it is also consuming too much of staff free time. Student punishment, when it reaches the proportions visited on Jake, is brutal; and I believe could be mentally dangerous if the wrong student is involved. The main reason though is that I am going to be near Jake's university wherever that is."

"Thanks Mike, that is pretty frank. What about you Chris?"

"The same objections as Mike, and in my case, Justin. I think there should be a staff representative that liaises with the Chairman as well. Without detracting from his position, the Chairman is usually going to be a teenager who wouldn't hurt for a little guidance when making decisions that could have far-reaching consequences. Shall we say a steadying hand when his youth might make some decisions—bad ones?"

"I am going to make Scottie the Chairman for the next year. If you remain, Chris, I would like to appoint you staff representative on the board, with a first remit to overhaul staff and student punishment and accessibility rules. For both of you I can guarantee that Justin and Jake will be accepted at Princeton, on fully funded scholarships, for the next four years to study for degrees in History in Justin's case and Finance for Jake."

Chris looked sharply at Mike. They were in Plainsboro, just a hop skip and a jump from Princeton.

"I am not intending to increase the salary of either of you because your bonuses already make you the highest-paid teachers in the school. Oh, one last thing, Chris. If you will take on the role of assistant soccer coach there will be a significant one of payment to you."

Chris looked at Mike and shrugged. Mike just mimicked Chris.

"I would like to have a private discussion with Mike and with Scottie before giving you our decisions."

"That is fine Chris, but I would like to leave the college before dinner. I have another meeting this evening."

"That should be doable."

Chris stood, thanked Duncan and left with Mike. They cornered Scottie and the three of them retired to Chris's apartment.

"Scottie, Duncan has told us that you are going to take over from Adam and will be reviewing staff and student punishment and accessibility rules. Can you tell us what your thoughts are on this?"

Scottie looked between the two teachers and then laid out his ideas.

"I think that students should still be able to vote on the competency of the teachers and render punishment as previously, but only at the end of the lesson in question. It shouldn't carry on to private time. Using the teachers for sex should still be allowed, but we really need to limit the times on this so that staff are not available for infinite numbers of hours. I'm only in favour of keeping this because teacher salaries are so high, and if students are going to have gay sex I think it is beneficial to have an older mentor. (Chris and Mike hadn't thought of that angle). Student punishment needs complete overhauling. What Adam allowed for Jake was totally irresponsible and potentially dangerous. If Mike hadn't remained every night during Jake's time, I would have stayed because I could see it was way over the top. I also believe that there should be at least one, preferably two staff reps on any committee set up to make recommendations and changes."

Chris looked at Mike.

"What do you think?"

"Honestly, Chris. My salary and bonuses this year are mouth-wateringly high. I could do with a few more years of this, and if the system is going to change and be more reasonable, I would be delighted to see Jake at Princeton, fully funded as well. The whole package for the two of us is unbeatable."

"I feel the same way. I know that Justin comes from money, but it is still a fantastic package for me as well. I don't think it can possibly be as bad next year and Justin and Jake won't be involved anyway. I say let's go for it, but with the caveat that the boys' university fees are paid even if we leave after one more year."

Effectively, deed done, and they took their decision back to Duncan.

"I am so delighted. I can't take you to dinner tonight but can I leave Scottie to arrange for the five of you to spend a weekend at my home early in your vacation time?"

Chris grinned.

"Is it likely to be like our last visit?"

Duncan grinned.

"It could be, but the intention this time is to take you all to dinner one night. The remainder of the stay, we can play it any way you would like."

With that he was gone, and Mike and Chris went to find their significant others to tell them the good news.

Before they all went off for summer vacation, Chris and Mike, Justin and Jake, had a final foursome. Part of that orgy was Justin and Jake watching as Chris made love to Mike. It took nearly an hour, and at the end of it Justin felt quite uncomfortable.

"Are you going to be making love to Mike like that when you are back here and Jake and I are at university?"

Chris wasn't stupid. That was a loaded question showing Justin's worry. He took his lover in a cuddle while he replied.

"I've loved Mike since I first set eyes on him at college. I'll probably love him for the remainder of my life. What we realised when Jake came on the scene was that Mike was capable of gay love and Jake was the man that brought him to that conclusion. Our love for each other had clouded the picture. The combination of finding you Justin, and Mike finding Jake, settled the problem for me. Mike and I can love each other without it being a romantic love. The lovemaking session you have just witnessed was my swan song with Mike. We may well have loads of foursomes when we get together, but I'm never going to make love to Mike again. We have sorted our future now, well, certainly the next four years of it. Mine is with you Jus, if you want me. I know that I love you very much and can see our future together now."

The kiss nearly had Mike and Jake's toes curling, and they were only watching it.

The summer was mapped out in some detail before they all left for vacation time. Time together, time with family, time as a foursome, one long weekend with Duncan when anything might happen. No silly vows of monogamy, only a vow to tell partners what they were doing.

They all returned to work/university on the same day, all four of them spending that first night in Chris's apartment for a fun-filled night that set the pattern of their lives together for the next four years, they hoped.

They all, of course, had separate sexual adventures during that time.

## Chapter 6

Chris and Mike had done quite a lot of prep work for the new semester while they were on holiday, so the first week before the students arrived they were able to take things easy. They spoke to their other halves and arranged the weekend. They had decided that although it would be easy to see each other, every night that was too disruptive. Instead they agreed weekends only, but not necessarily every weekend. School and Uni activities would intervene sometimes, particularly Chris' refereeing duties.

Scottie was back early as well and sent for Chris.

"Welcome back, Chris. I thought we could have an early meeting, to discuss the agenda for the first full meeting of the board to sort out staff and student punishment and accessibility."

"I would like that. I assume that now you are head honcho you would like me to call you Sir, in keeping with the existing rules."

"I think that would be best Chris, but in private I think we can stick with first names. I am, after all, going to be working closely with you this year."

That suited Chris.

"So what are we going to write into the rule book?"

"Student punishment first, I think. What happened to Jake mustn't be allowed to happen again. Student punishment is a rare event, so why don't we have a panel of three board members hear the case for punishment and rule on it when they have had time to consider the crime? We can set guidelines for them to follow, but I think that no punishment should drag on for more than one day. I also think that sexual and physical is fine, but nothing disgusting. Instrument for physical punishment should be a paddle, bloody painful but it won't cause damage if we set a sensible limit on the number that can be administered."

"What do you consider a sensible limit?"

"Fifteen."

"Why?"

"Twenty is too many Scottie, and ten isn't always enough. They should be administered five at a time with a short break in between."

Scottie nodded his agreement.

"What about sexual punishment?"

Chris smiled at that.

"Loads of it, if I am administering it."

Both of them laughed when Scottie came back very quickly with one word, "slut."

"Seriously, a board member should witness it and pull the plug if the recipient looks as though he may be traumatised by it. We should be looking for humiliation and embarrassment. Fun for the giver, definitely not for the receiver."

Scottie liked that.

"I will put that to the board at our first meeting, and you should be there as well. Now, what about staff?"

"Similar system I think, except that, as it usually takes place immediately after a lesson, the class leader should make the decision and it can be the same as student punishment."

"And accessibility?"

"Staff should be free after dinner in the evenings, and all weekend, except where they have duties, like the sports coach and me, refereeing. Between end of instruction and dinner they will need to do tutorials. If they have any free time after that then students can use them for sex. My experience last year was that it wasn't too obtrusive after the new boys had got over the novelty. Most of you guys prefer sex with your own crowd. Mike and I were probably used the most because of our age, and in my case it was fun and not a chore. Mike will probably be the same this year, now that he has recognised his sexuality. Both of us have cleared it with our lovers. I think it should be made clear that anything disgusting, like water sports, are definitely out."

Scottie was happy with all of that and the agenda for the first meeting was simply those two subjects.

Chris was introduced to all of the new class leaders at the first meeting, and re-acquainted with the old ones that were still at the Academy. He thought one of the new ones, Kilo, might be trouble for him, judging by his first comment.

"I thought this school was run by the students, so what is a teacher doing here?"

Scottie stepped in then.

"It was considered a good idea to have the steadying influence of a mature member of the academy, and Duncan thought Chris was ideal for the appointment."

"He'll probably just try to water down staff punishment and accessibility."

Scottie laughed. "I'm sure he will. Let's get on, shall we?"

Student punishment, as suggested by Scottie, was waived through almost on a nod. No one wanted that to get heavy. The staff one was a battle, mostly because Kilo wanted much more severe punishment over a longer period, and more sex time allowed. He didn't win because most of the other class leaders realised that keeping the staff sweet was likely to be good for their grades. Chris' input had been almost nil, having sorted it with Scottie previously. That was probably the main reason there was so little dissention at Scottie's proposals, but Kilo obviously resented the limitations. Unfortunately for Chris, Kilo was in one of his history classes and quickly showed how he was going to deal with him.

A complete new class, so Chris did his intro having become proficient at it in this his third year.

"Now gentlemen, please retain the same seats as you presently occupy until I have got used to you. Commencing at the back left hand corner of the class, will you stand up one at a time and introduce yourselves. Name, age and a potted history."

Kilo objected on the grounds that the potted history was unnecessary.

"I don't intend wasting teaching time arguing my methods with you, Sir. If you have any problems we can discuss them in free time. Now continue please."

During the course of the lesson Kilo interrupted several more times gaining the same answer. By the end of the lesson Kilo was steaming, and the remainder of the class were pissed off with him.

"I think the whole approach to this lesson was unsatisfactory Lovell, so I'm going to punish you."

There were a lot of very antagonistic looks aimed at Kilo.

"To start with, get naked."

Chris didn't argue because he realised he would only make it worse.

"Now get an erection and display."

No one objected to that. There were plenty of gasps and complimentary voices heard when Chris was displayed.

"Prostrate yourself over the desk and spread your legs as wide as you can get them."

Kilo walked up to the desk then and stood at the side so that the whole class could see. He made Chris suck on all the fingers of one hand before introducing them one at a time to Chris's anus.

"Huh. He's obviously been a shitty teacher before. He is quite slack."

Pointing at two other students, he spoke to them.

"Stand either side of him and use a hand to spread his cheeks wider."

Chris felt humiliated. This was unjustified punishment with a completely new class.

When Kilo had all five digits of one hand pushing hard inside Chris, he rotated them before pulling them out and standing back to undress. He was already erect, and with minimum spit on his cock, he pushed it straight into Chris all the way.

"Perhaps I can fuck some teaching ability into you," was his comment as he fucked Chris to orgasm with a more than acceptable cock—in normal circumstances, but not when it was barely lubricated.

"That wasn't bad, slut, I might do that after every lesson. Now someone fetch me the paddle, he is going to take the maximum strokes, as hard as I can make them."

Jeff Laker had read the school rules and punishment details for staff and students. He thought that Kilo would render too much pain with fifteen strokes, besides which he didn't consider Chris had done anything wrong. He slid out of the classroom and found Scottie. As quickly as he could he explained what was happening.

Back in the classroom, Kilo had Chris on his desk on his back with two students holding his legs well back and wide. You could see cum running out of his arse, being spread over it by the paddle that had already connected twice. Scottie heard both screams as he started to run. He opened the classroom door just in time to see Kilo swing the paddle for the third stroke. The power behind it was stupefying. Scottie ran to the front and wrenched the paddle from Kilo's hand and screamed at him.

"Go and pack, be out of this Academy before dark."

He could see that Chris was in serious distress.

"Jeff, run and get the medic. Bring back a stretcher with you."

Turning to the two students still holding Chris's legs he told them, "Roll him over onto his tummy and make him as comfortable as you can."

He gasped when he saw Chris's butt. It looked terrible.

While they waited, Scottie got the whole story.

"Teacher punishment was never intended to be like this. You know the limits, but it isn't meant to be brutal. We all know you can get very sexual with the teachers and that is accepted, but brutal use of the paddle is not acceptable."

The medic came in, transferred Chris to the stretcher and he was taken to the school infirmary. Scottie remained with him until the nurse had treated his bottom and put him to sleep. He went back to his office, summoned Jeff Laker and made him class leader. Then he phoned Duncan to tell him what he had done. Mike was informed and the decision left to him whether Justin was told or not.

Heading out for dinner, Scottie's thought was, *'I hope I don't have too many incidents like that, otherwise I might follow Kilo out of the door.'* That made him think and he checked with security that Kilo had in fact left the premises. He hadn't. Duncan had called security and told them to detain Kilo until he arrived the next morning.

Kilo was paraded before the whole academy the next morning, naked. A bench had been brought in from the gym and he was secured to it face down. Mike was considered the best individual to render punishment; but before that, four teachers, known to be well-endowed, were invited to fuck him to orgasm. Then Mike administered fifteen strokes of the paddle in groups of five. Punishment complete and Duncan threw his clothes at him.

"Your bags are at the main gate. Leave now. And if you ever mention anything about this academy to another soul, I will have you found and you will be punished like this every day until I am satisfied that you know you have done wrong."

Kilo was in so much pain, but terrified of what might happen if he didn't disappear. Duncan addressed the audience.

"Students. You know that I am giving you all a second chance where you have previously failed. Staff, you know that this is the best teaching post any of you will ever get. You live in luxury, are paid well and the only down side is that you can be punished and have sex forced upon you. If any of you think you can get better than this, please inform admin and you can leave now with no penalty for breach of contract."

Of course, no one left and things returned to normal. Even straight members of staff would put up with gay sex for all the plusses that this post gave them. Twenty four hours later, a much bruised Chris was back at his post teaching. Nobody commented on the fact that he didn't sit down in class for about a week, and Jeff was his first booked tutorial.

"I don't really want tutoring Chris. Your lessons are too good to need it. I just wanted to get to know you a little better now that I am class leader."

Chris had read the history of this student and was surprised he had failed at his last school.

"I notice you are only eighteen, Sir, so before you start on me, can I ask why you failed at your last school?"

"I come from Alabama and I'm gay. That is probably sufficient information for you."

Chris nodded. He couldn't even begin to understand the stress this boy was under keeping his sexuality a secret.

"It is and I'm sorry that it has cost you two years of your life effectively. We will make up for it here though, and you'll go to a first class university."

"Thanks Chris. Before I hear about you, will you strip for me? I'd like to see how the bruising is on your butt."

Chris knew he could just have dropped his pants, so his guess was that Jeff wanted more than a look. He undressed stood in front of this very cute student and then turned round and adopted the display stance until told otherwise. He felt the soft hand stroke his cheeks. It felt good.

"Are you still using cream on it?"

"Yes; morning, noon and night. It is very good stuff. I think there is an anaesthetic in it."

"If you get it for me now and go to your bed to lay down, I'll do it for you tonight."

Chris could have said he was quite capable of doing it, but this boy patently wanted to do it, and he was cute. Jeff did an excellent job naturally bringing Chris to a very hard erection. Jeff made him turn over when he was finished and saw the hard cock.

"Can I get rid of that for you, Chris?"

Chris could see the longing in the boy's eyes, so he nodded, and then said:

"If you would like to strip, it would be my pleasure to get rid of that bulge in your trousers as well."

Jeff blushed, which Chris found endearing and made him determined to pull out the stop in satisfying this boy.

Jeff had a wonderful little boy look about him, and when he was naked, Chris' eyes watered. The boy was gorgeous. Not particularly buffed, but a pleasant body with a very attractive groin: a gorgeous six-inch cock and a low slung ball sac. The cruncher though was the shy smile that said everything.

*'Giving him a first class blowjob will be no trouble at all,'* was his thought.

"On the bed with me then, Sir."

Jeff blushed at being called Sir in these circumstances.

"You don't have to call me Sir in here, Chris."

"Okay Lovely Boy, when I get to your groin you can start on my cock. Until then, just enjoy."

A few gentle lip kisses followed that before Chris worked his way down the boy's body, exciting the nipples as he went. At the groin he licked the balls first, supporting them in the palm of one hand. Then he moved up the shaft until he could take the head in his mouth to worry it with his tongue while sucking gently on it. He felt Jeff start to reciprocate, tentatively at first, but then with more surety. It clicked then that Jeff had little or no experience of gay sex. He determined then to make this blowjob last as long as possible. The result was a little boy crying in his arms after his orgasm, swearing to be his slave forever. Chris was so pleased that he had fully satisfied this angel and kissed and caressed him gently while he calmed down.

*'I wish all my tutorials could be this satisfying,'* was his thought.

Dressed and sat back in the lounge, Jeff looked at Chris from hooded eyes and spoke.

"Thank you for that, Sir. May I come back another night for you to make love to me completely? No one has ever made me feel this good. I would so like to learn from you."

"I think I would like that very much."

"You don't have to, Sir. Only do it if you would like to."

Chris slid across the floor and took Jeff's face in his hands before kissing him several times, finishing with one that made his toes curl.

"Believe me, I would like to. I think you are enchanting."

Jeff's smile was worth every minute of the last hour.

"And remember, it is me that has to call you Sir, not the other way round."

Chris was smiling as he said it and Jeff realised what he had been doing and giggled.

"In my mind you'll always be Sir, because you are so special as a teacher, both in the classroom and the bedroom."

That was good enough for Chris and he saw his little munchkin out before leaving for the staff restaurant with a tale for Mike.

"Another adventure, Chris. Are you going to tell Justin?"

Chris looked shocked that Mike would even ask.

"Of course. If I start withholding that kind of information it will soon become outright lies and that will be it. End of my happiness. I want Justin with me forever now that I have found him."

Mike was so pleased that he had not misjudged his best friend.

"I'm the same. There is a little cutie in one of my classes. I know I am going to take him to bed if I get the chance, but I really live for my times with Jake."

Two friends renewed their trust, love, and respect for each other with that conversation.

Chris's conversation with Justin that night was fun. Justin thought it was cute that Chris was going to be teaching this little southern boy the finer points of gay sex.

"Would you like to have a final exam for him? I'll be delighted to be the examiner."

That was greeted with hoots of laughter until Chris got serious and told his love.

"No chance, you might fall in love with him and then I'd lose you."

"That isn't going to happen with any other man, ever. Love you, see you Friday night."

That was it. All calm on the love front.

The next night, Jeff came to see Chris after the evening meal. This was going to be more than just sex, and Chris knew it. Jeff was a seriously cute kid, almost gagging to learn more about gay sex with this sexy history teacher. There was a huge dollop of lust in Chris' thinking, but he did genuinely like Jeff so the lovemaking would be special.

Chris took the boy's virginity that night, and the look of wonder on his face after he orgasmed made it certain in Chris' mind that the boy had enjoyed the experience. There was no doubt in his mind that Jeff would never give him any grief as class leader, not that students did in general, because he was good at his job.

Life settled down after a couple of weeks. There was quite a lot of heavy sexual use of staff that tailed off as expected. Chris and Mike bore the brunt of that because they were the youngest, and sexiest members of staff. Chris loved it and Mike tolerated it. Their weekends were full of sex as well, but in both cases it was with their true loves.

# Chapter 7

Mike came to see Chris on the Thursday evening after dinner.

"I couldn't talk about this at dinner, Chris, but I'm seriously worried."

Chris could see the worry on his friends face and asked him why.

"I don't know where my mind was this afternoon but I delivered a pathetic lecture. My class leader was so incensed that instead of just specifying punishment he polled the whole class. Every student voted for punishment. I have to admit looking back on it, it was awful."

Mike shrugged before continuing.

"Damien as class leader could have specified instant punishment but he wants to run it by the board asking for one hour after lessons tomorrow. He says he is going to seek permission for 50 minutes of sexual abuse followed by a punishment of 10 medium with the paddle. He wants leeway to take five extras, hard. I think he'll get it with a unanimous vote from the class."

What Mike didn't mention, even to his best friend, was why he had been so bad.

Chris knew he would be asked to sit in on this one and would, of course, have liked to reduce it; but in all honesty, if Mike was as bad as he said, there would be no justification in doing so. He knew that this would be a monstrously humiliating session for Mike because Jake would be waiting for him afterwards. The only thing he could hope for was a deferment of punishment until Monday.

At the meeting, Scottie wasn't vindictive, having great respect for Mike and Chris, but he couldn't see the justification in delaying it.

"I'm sorry Chris, but it will go ahead as planned at 5 o'clock today. You and I will witness."

Chris felt slightly relieved, at least he would be there if Mike got into trouble mentally.

In the two+ years that Chris had been at the academy he realised he had never heard of an out-of-classroom punishment of a member of staff. Well, not a legal one anyway. He was incredulous when he entered the gymnasium at ten to five to find equipment he didn't even know existed. The punishment bench was like nothing he had seen before. It looked like a slightly elongated padded stool, except that it was a bit lower and the legs spread to about 2 ½ feet with restraints on one set of legs and a spreader bar fixed to the other set of legs with restraints on the end. Next to it was a piece of equipment that every gay man must have seen. A doctor's examination table with stirrups fitted for internal examination of females, but also incredibly useful to splay a male ready for fucking or beating. On a table next to that were several dildos of varying sizes, a tube of gel and a paddle— unusually, there was also a cane. Chris immediately protested at the cane.

"Scottie, we agreed that canes would not be used as a punishment tool."

"Standard kit, Chris, but I will not allow it to be used."

Chris nodded with satisfaction and then almost turned white as the gym door opened and Jake walked in.

"Jake, what are you doing here? I thought you would have remained in Mike's apartment."

"Scottie thought an old boy as witness to this staff punishment would be a good idea. So did I. Teachers being punished should be interesting. I've left a note for Mike, he isn't back yet."

"He isn't back because he is the member of staff being punished."

Jake was obviously quite shocked so Chris continued.

"We don't have time now. I'll tell all when it is finished."

The doors opened again and Mike walked in escorted by his class leader. He was still fully clothed. The remainder of the class followed. So it looked like the class would watch and take part, no doubt, and the witnesses would be the board Chairman, Scottie, the staff representative, Chris, and the ex-student, Jake.

The master for this was Damien, the class leader. He was reputed to have ten thick inches of circumcised penis. Chris hoped that wasn't true because he was sure it would find a hole sometime during the proceedings.

The dais from the end of the gym had been moved to the centre so that the class could spread all-round it. Damien asked Chris, Scottie and Jake to stand at one side of the dais, making that side the centre of his operation.

Mike was stood facing his lover, his best friend and the board Chairman.

Damien spoke then.

"Mike, you have been found guilty of delivering a seriously inept lecture that has garnered the unanimous vote of the class for punishment. The board and staff representative have agreed that my punishment is acceptable. For the next 50 minutes your class will be allowed to show you how upset they are at this failure on your part, after which I will administer ten medium strength strokes of the paddle. It has further been agreed that if you fail to co-operate completely at any time during the hour, I may use the cane for a further five strokes."

Chris looked at Scottie who just shrugged.

Mike was devastated even before it started, knowing that Jake was going to witness it.

"Now Mike, strip and display."

Mike's superb body was a complete turn on for every man in the room. Jake blushed because he was obviously erect as well.

"Now, fist yourself to an erection."

Mike did, but he was patently very embarrassed doing so.

"Jazz and Peter, punishment bench."

The two boys moved the bench onto the raised dais.

Everyone was curious how this was going to work. What they saw when Damien had completed the operation was almost too much for the gay boys. Mike was bent over the padded section, his legs fixed into the spreader bar at almost maximum stretch, and his wrists in the other restraints. The position served to have his cheeks spread so wide that his anus was clearly displayed.

Damien spanked him barehanded, two to each cheek, before slicking up fingers and commencing a finger-fuck, escalating from one finger to all five digits on one hand. He was stood at the side so that everyone, by moving round could see the action.

"Jazz and Peter, use one hand on each cheek and spread his anus more. Let everyone see what will be made available to them shortly."

Mike wanted to cry. The humiliation was mind-bending.

Damien picked up one of the dildos then. It was a ten incher. He lubed it but then introduced it to Mike's anus, sliding it all the way in, smoothly. He released Mike then and had him stand at display with his arse facing the three witnesses. Jazz and Peter removed the bench and brought the examination table onto the dais. Mike was secured into it with his legs wound well back and again spread very wide. The dildo was still fully embedded in his arse.

"The senior man present is the Chairman. Scottie, would you do us the honour of fucking our delinquent teacher to orgasm?"

Scottie didn't want to but he didn't want to embarrass a leader by refusing, so he stripped, lubed his penis and withdrew the dildo from Mike's arse before sliding in and commencing a slow fuck to orgasm. He loved it, but would much sooner have done it in a bed in private. He so admired Mike for his ability and his physicality. Mike came as well. Scottie had been so gentle and erotic.

The tears flowed now. Mike knew that Jake had seen him orgasm and he thought that was monstrous, even if it was Scottie who he respected, and in all honesty, lusted after a little as well.

Damien went next and everyone gasped. They had no idea he carried such an impressive weapon between his legs. Scottie equalled him in length at 10 inches, but Damien beat him by a couple of inches at least in girth. Mike would definitely feel that when it entered him. That was a truism. Damien fucked for longevity, long and slow. He had Mike almost serial orgasming, it was amazing. The assault on his prostate was nonstop.

Four other boys fucked Mike before Scottie indicated that was enough.

The punishment bench was brought up again and Mike was strapped over it to receive ten strokes of the paddle in sets of five.

At the end of the session he stood in front of his class and apologised for his poor performance and hoped they would forgive him. Then he was helped out of the gym by Chris and Jake and taken to his apartment where he disintegrated in heartrending sobs. He clung to Jake, pleading to be forgiven.

"That's ridiculous, Mike. There is nothing to forgive. I love you so much. I'm always going to love you."

Chris could see that Jake was handling the situation and left.

"Call me if you need me," was his parting comment.

Jake treated Mike like a baby after that. He took him for a shower, washed him gently and tucked him into bed when he had stopped crying, not for one second failing to remind him that he was loved and always would be.

He sat in the lounge thinking after that, wondering how Mike would feel in the morning. The entry bell rang and Jake answered it. Scottie was at the door looking worried.

"How is he Jake?"

Jake shook his head.

"I don't know. Physically, I am sure he is fine. The sex and the punishment were reasonable. It was the humiliation that hit him. I don't know what he will be like in the morning. This could be very bad for him."

"Please let me know if there is anything I can do. I will alert Duncan at the university just in case."

Jake was left to himself then, and decided to have an early night as well and slid into the bed to cuddle his lover.

The next morning, Mike looked hunted. He wouldn't look at Jake.

"It's okay, Mike. Just let it go. Everyone admires you, even the class that punished you."

"I let them down, Jake, because I couldn't control my emotions. My dad died on Wednesday, which was why I was distracted. I should have gone home to my mum instead of teaching a class."

Jake was shocked.

"Well why don't you go home today?"

"Not necessary now. I'll go home for the funeral and stay a couple of days to help mum."

Jake informed Chris and Scottie and then spent the weekend pampering his lover. Mike remained very quiet for the weekend, not connecting with Jake or Chris at all.

Jake was worried returning to university on Monday and Chris was even more worried because he didn't see Mike before first lesson. Scottie interrupted that lesson to ask Chris if Mike had already left for home.

"He hasn't checked out, Chris, and he hasn't informed anyone that he wouldn't be taking his first lesson."

Chris gave his class a reading exercise and accompanied Scottie to Mike's apartment. There was no answer, so Scottie used his master key. What they saw on entry made Chris scream an agonising 'no'.

Mike was hanging from a rope attached to the beam in his lounge, a toppled chair at his feet. They cut him down and Chris was about to start mouth to mouth resuscitation when he realised Mike was quite cold.

He turned to Scottie, reverting to little boy mode.

"Why Scottie, why would he do something like this? He had everything to live for."

Scottie was too young to put it all together while he was in shock as well. He just shook his head, but had the sense to call 911 for police and ambulance.

They were both numb with shock when both emergency services arrived and were taken to the police precinct while the body was removed to the morgue.

Chris couldn't speak. The shock was just too immense, but Scottie eventually managed to tell the police all he knew, which wasn't much when he had edited out the staff punishment. Fortunately, the case was deemed a simple suicide caused by the shock of the deceased father dying.

The fallout over the next few weeks left a pall of misery over the academy. Mike had been a popular teacher. That one lapse had been punished according to the rules without anyone seeking the reason. Everyone concerned felt awful, especially Chris who felt betrayed that Mike hadn't confided in him, or Jake, come to that. *'Why ever not'* was his question.

The remainder of that semester was a nightmare for Jake, Justin and Chris. Justin and Chris tried so hard to include Jake in everything, even taking him to bed with them every night at the weekend. Sex was never a factor and that led to both Chris and Justin almost reaching overload in frustration. Jake was inconsolable, and at semester end Chris and Justin took him with them. In all honesty, they were worried about his mental state. He had loved Mike fiercely and nothing appeared to bring him out of his sadness. The new semester started and Jake slowly came out of his grief, but he never stopped asking the question, 'Why?' No one would ever know the answer to that.

The major breakthrough in his normalisation came just before half term when Justin called Chris mid-week.

"Guess what Lover?"

Laughing at such a silly question, Chris replied.

"You have graduated three years early and have been selected for a solo flight to the moon."

It was a good feeling to be laughing and joking again.

"No, much better than that. I took Jake to bed last night and made love to him. He cried happy tears after wards. I think we have made it, Chris. He is almost back to normal. I even heard him laugh a couple of days ago."

Chris breathed a sigh of relief.

"Bring him with you at the weekend and we'll smother him in love. Next step will be to find him a new boyfriend."

Enough said, but the weekend was a blast. Loads of threesomes with Jake being at the centre of attention, and unbridled laughter for the first time in months.

"I love you guys. I would never have made it this far without you."

Chris surprised the others then when he replied.

"I don't think I would have made it without you either. I loved Mike so much that I thought I would never recover from losing my best friend. Even Justin's love couldn't lift the pall that hung over me, but I saw a greater need in you, so it was bringing you back to the world that brought me back as well."

Justin could have felt hurt by that admission but he knew the love that existed between Chris and Mike and had never resented it.

Looking as cheeky as he could, Justin spoke.

"Now we have to find him a boyfriend Chris, or we learn to live as a threesome."

It was said seriously and both Chris and Jake looked thoughtfully at him. That idea didn't warrant anymore discussion at this point in time, but it sure as hell generated a load of thinking from all three.

Chris continued to make love to Jeff a couple of times a week. The boy was just so receptive and delightful to play with. Justin didn't mind and admitted that he and Jake were doing the same. The natural progression had been Jeff joining them some weekends and the lovemaking became a spectator sport quite frequently. Chris and Justin realised that the best sessions of all were when they could watch Jake and Jeff make love properly on Chris's bed. It invariably made them both so horny that Jake and Jeff were treated to the reverse when they finished.

Chris asked Jeff if he really enjoyed Jake making love to him, and didn't he ever feel like being the top as Jake was so close to same age as him.

"Oh no Chris, I don't ever want to be the top unless it was to please you. Jake and Justin are nice, but it's you that I love."

*'Oh shit,'* was Chris's thought, this wasn't what he wanted. He didn't let his words or actions give away that thought, instead he cuddled his little munchkin and made a suggestion.

"Well I would like you to make love to me and fuck me, because, to round out your sex education, you need to experience being the top even if it is only the once."

Chris almost cried with pleasure when the action took place. Jeff was so gentle and unsure of himself. It was pure magic.

The ideal situation now would be for Jeff and Jake to become an item. Although there was only two years between them in biological age, in maturity that stretched to many more. Jake had matured enormously coping with the trauma of Mike's punishments and then his subsequent suicide, while Jeff was really still an innocent abroad.

Justin had a different worry. He loved Chris like he never believed he would love another man, but he was also beginning to love Jake. They had become much closer, initially while he helped Jake overcome the loss of Mike, and then because they realised they had a lot in common, not the least of which was fantastic empathy with each other when they made love.

Jake was still carrying a huge chunk of love for Mike and wasn't yet realising that he and Justin were gelling more all the time.

The last of the three to worry about was Jeff. He was just head over heels in love with Chris. Part of that was hero worship of a superb teacher who made his subject come alive, where so many made it boring. The other part was, of course, the amazing ability that Chris had as a lover. He managed to take Jeff off to Paradise within minutes of them starting to make love, and it was a rare session where he didn't have multiple orgasms. Yes, he had found it exciting to make love to Chris the once, but he had no wish to do it again, and Jake had been 'nice,' but that was all. He liked having Justin and Jake as friends, but the sex with them was only because Chris wanted it.

Over time, Justin realised the situation more than Chris, who was blinded by his love for Justin. The crunch came at the end of the semester.

Jeff really had nowhere to go. He was frightened to go home where he was sure his sexuality would show, having enjoyed a period of gay sex and a love for Chris. Justin suggested that Chris take him home with him as the holiday was only a couple of weeks.

"It's logical, Lover. Jake needs somewhere to go as well so he can come home with me and Jeff with you. We are lucky having understanding parents."

It dawned on Chris at last.

"You're in love with Jake, aren't you?"

Justin looked as guilty as hell so there was no point in denying it.

"I'm sorry Chris, but yes, I am. The problem is I'm still just as much in love with you as I ever was. I know that sounds daft, but I am. Also, I can see that Jeff thinks that you are the sun and the moon. The only completely logical thing to do is to become a foursome, and that is totally illogical. Yes I know, logical, illogical. So what is the solution so that no one gets hurt?"

It all came together for Chris then. What he felt for Jeff was love as well. He and Justin now had a huge problem. They both loved each other but the complication in loving the other two was the protective element. Justin and he were the mature ones nurturing their chicks. The love was just as intense, but different.

Delayed solution really, by going with Justin's idea for the holiday.

Chris' parents fell in love with Jeff almost on sight. He was such a little charmer. When they asked Chris what had happened to Justin, he had to tell them half the truth. Jake still needed Justin's strength while he came to terms with Mike's death, and in Jeff's case, he needed a more mature male to help him sort out his sexuality.

Dad made the position of the parents clear.

"Well, you make sure you look after him. We think he is delightful."

The two weeks of the holiday really clarified the love situation. Chris had been totally enamoured with Jeff having his company 24/7 for the two weeks. Yes he had missed Justin, but it wasn't with the intensity of old that he could have expected. Justin had been good for Jake and they returned to university, Jake showing more independence and self-confidence. Weekends became a couple of times a month instead of every weekend, and the mid-week telephone calls tailed off as well.

It began to look as though everything was settling down with the new pairings. The academic year ended. Jeff went home with Chris again, and Chris and Justin accepted that they were now just loving friends with benefits. Jeff's results were as expected and he joined Justin and Jake at university for the next semester. Chris returned to the academy for another year and was met by a new face.

# Chapter 8

"Chris Lovell, I'm Iain Rush. Duncan's brother."

"Hello Iain, I'm pleased to meet you."

"I am taking over the academy from Duncan. He graduated and is now in England at Oxford University. You are the senior teacher now so we will be liaising with each other no doubt. I have called a meeting of all new and existing class leaders for 1400 today. I would like you to attend so that you can inform all other staff members of the new regime."

"Very well. I'll get settled back in and see you after lunch."

Chris turned to leave and Iain spoke again.

"Oh, and by the way. I expect to be called Sir, the same as the class leaders."

The tone of voice alerted Chris to a more serious regime to be expected.

"I won't forget, Sir."

At the meeting, Chris was introduced to the new class leaders. One of his history class leaders was definitely a no-nonsense individual—he showed Chris his character straight away.

No hand shake, just the terse comment.

"I'm Adam Lithgow. I expect nothing but the best from you for the next two years, and like the Chairman, I expect to be called Sir, at all times. Slip up and your arse will know how I feel about it."

Chris looked the boy up and down and nodded.

"I understand, Sir."

*'This one is trouble,'* was his thought. He checked out the stats on the student database. Adam was eighteen, another dropout that had wasted two years of his life being a hard arse. He and Iain had been together so Chris guessed they were friends. He ran checks on all the new students he would have to deal with so that he could streamline introduction. The first lesson with Adam's class set the tone for the year.

"Good morning, gentlemen. My name is Chris Lovell, I will be your history teacher for this year. I already know all your names and the potted history in your student files, so, I just need to put the faces to the names. Will you please, sit in the same seat each lesson until I get to know you. Starting at the back left, will you in turn, stand up and give me your name."

"Just get on with it Teach, stop wasting time."

Chris considered Adam while he thought.

"Until I am relieved of this post, Sir, we will do things the same tried and successful way I have done since I graduated college. If you have any issues with my methods, please feel free to see me after instruction."

Before Chris could continue, Adam spoke again.

"Let's get the hierarchy in this class sorted. To remind you who is in charge, strip, naked. You will be naked for all my classes until told otherwise."

Chris knew he had to obey and very slowly took off all his clothes. He was determined now that this class would not get his best instruction, and he would not progress them as fast as the others. He was still blushing with embarrassment even though this was not new to him.

Stood naked in front of the class, he tried to ignore his nudity and the eyes of all the class scoping him out. He pointed to two boys in the front row.

"You and you, take a pile of the books on my desk and distribute them to each student."

"Do your own distribution, Teach."

Chris knew now how to waste times. He slowly delivered the books, returned to his seat and pretended to look through his notes.

"Open the books and write your name on the inside cover. Do so with all subsequent distributions. Today we start with American history from the time of the Pilgrim Fathers."

Chris laboured every point he made during the lecture and covered only about half of what he would do normally. At the end of the lesson he expected a negative response from Adam and wasn't disappointed.

"Lousy lesson, Teach, bend over your desk and let me show you my displeasure."

Chris took five quite hard slaps from Adam's bare hand.

"You need to improve rapidly."

And then he was gone. Chris dressed quickly before the next class entered. The remainder of his new classes went as planned and Chris realised that Adam's class would soon realise in conversation with friends that they were falling well behind.

The next lesson with Adam's class was much like the first one. Chris was not allowed to use other students to speed up anything. At the end of the lesson, it being the last of the day, Adam used the extra time available to further humiliate Chris.

"That was another waste of time, Teach. I think you might need a protein injection. Get on your knees and suck my cock to orgasm, swallow all my cum."

Chris really pissed Adam off by complying with no hesitation. He dropped to his knees, reached up immediately to release Adam's belt and unzip his trousers. He lowered trousers and underwear together and immediately took the flaccid cock in his mouth. Adam was furious and face-fucked Chris once he had a hard cock, making him gag frequently because he carried a monster between his legs. Orgasm achieved and he pushed Chris away from him.

"Lousy blowjob, I guess you'll be doing a lot of that until you are much better."

Chris returned to his apartment to consider what he could do to curb this nasty piece of work. Iain was the only person who could do anything and Chris had the idea he wouldn't.

He carried out two tutorials that evening on members of Adam's class and was requested at the end to give them blowjobs as well. They were nice kids with good manners. The results were two very satisfied customers.

"Thanks, Chris. The instruction was great, as were the blowjobs."

Similar comment from both—and the thought that Adam was making things bad in the classroom, affecting quality of teaching.

Satisfactory tutorials soon had more of the class finding Adam a disrupting influence and they started telling him to shut up and let Chris do his job. The more this happened, the nastier Adam became. He saw his chance to really humiliate Chris when he caught him refereeing a soccer match one Saturday afternoon. With nothing much else to do on Saturday afternoons, the match was well attended. Many of the students only knew Chris from the sports fields if they didn't take history.

Iain was at the match and Adam approached him with his idea.

"Hi, Iain."

"Oh, hi Adam, how are lessons going?"

"Apart from history, very well, but Lovell is a complete waste of space with my class. I thought we might use this match to really show him my displeasure."

"Okay, what do you have in mind?"

"I thought we could have him referee, naked. Then, as a reward for anyone scoring a goal, he could give them a blowjob. He could start at one goal and work to the other end so that everyone got a good look. I'm sure the goal scorers would be happy."

Iain thought that was pushing things a little, but he okay-ed it. He thought Chris had an awesome body, having seen him in the gym a few times. He had thought about taking him back to his apartment to fuck him, but that was probably pushing the limits of the staff contract unless he had an excuse. Perhaps he would get one here.

When Chris blew up for a foul, Adam trotted onto the field and talked to him.

"We have decided to up the entertainment value for the spectators and reward the goal scorers. Take off all of your clothes. When the next guy scores you are to offer him a blow job. Start at the goal scorer's end and move towards the other end at intervals so that everyone gets a good look."

Chris protested that this was going too far.

"This is punishment for your poor performance in the classroom and has been sanctioned by the Chairman."

Chris disrobed, keeping on just his socks and boots. There were plenty of cheers when the game restarted. Chris felt so humiliated that his refereeing deteriorated and he started getting booed. Iain took advantage then and walked onto the pitch with a cane.

"Your performance is pathetic. Bend over, legs well spread."

Chris obeyed and gasped as the first of ten quite hard strokes of the cane landed.

His performance got worse then, and at half time he told one of the linesmen to referee the reminder of the game. He would run the line.

Iain and Adam were angry when the game resumed and determined to up the humiliation at the end. Meanwhile, Chris had to give three very public blowjobs to the goal scorers in the second half.

At the end of the game, Iain ran onto the pitch with Adam, carrying a loud hailer.

"Everyone who would like to see the referee punished for his pathetic performance gather round."

There was a large circle round Iain, Adam and Chris.

"Team captains please join us. Iain and I are going to tag team fucking the referee for his pathetic performance. The captains may do so after us to show their displeasure."

A bench was brought onto the field and Chris was stretched across it, legs as wide as they would go. The spectators watched as Adam hooked his T shirt over his head and then undid his cut down jeans before allowing them to fall open revealing his monster cock almost erect. With very little spit on it he fisted himself to a full erection, eliciting gasps from the audience, before sliding it over Chris's sphincter. Chris screamed at the pain but Adam went in all the way before starting a long slow fuck. After about five minutes he swapped with Iain. It took them nearly half an hour to cum, and then the team captains repeated it. At the end, Chris was in so much pain that two staff members carried him to the infirmary.

After being examined and treated by the nurse, Chris was told that if he was penetrated again before he had healed he may well be permanently damaged. That message was carried to Iain by a staff member.

Chris returned to his apartment, showered and dropped into bed. On Sunday he didn't get out of bed except to empty his bladder and his bowels. Monday morning he turned up for his first lesson looking very ill. At the end of the class he looked worse because he had given several blowjobs and been spanked for poor performance, at Adam's instigation of course. Another staff member saw him at the end of the lesson and escorted him back to the infirmary where he was put to bed under the supervision of the nurse. Iain stormed in when the news got to him.

"I want that malingerer in his classroom, like now."

"He is going nowhere except hospital. I have already sent for an ambulance."

The nurse said nothing else and Iain left to think about what he could do.

Jeff, Justin and Jake turned up at the hospital as soon as the news reached them. Justin, after the doctor had told him the story, telephoned Duncan in England and repeated it to him.

"When he is fit enough to be released he is going home to his parents to recuperate and for us to consider his next actions. This staff punishment and humiliation is getting out of hand with your brother and this creep Adam Lithgow upping the stakes all the time. Standards of instruction are dropping as staff become more resentful. You need to consider what you want from this academy, because at the end of this school year I imagine most of the best teachers will be moving on."

Duncan had tried so hard to get his brother to behave and he knew that Adam was a bad influence on him. First move, get rid of Adam from the student body.

Job done, but Iain rebelled again. Duncan felt he had no choice now if his dream wasn't to collapse. He dismissed Iain, cut off his allowance and told him to go out and get a job. Then he spoke to Chris.

"I am so sorry for the way my brother has subverted my intentions, Chris, and that you have been on the receiving end of his and Adam's sadism. I know I shouldn't even consider asking this favour of you, but I don't see any alternative if I am to keep the academy alive in the form I originally planned. When you are released from hospital, will you return to the academy as Chairman? I will not expect you to carry out anything other than light duties until you are ready to return to full work. During your time on light duties, will you assess all the student leaders to find a new deputy Chairman? Spread your search wider if you need to the remainder of the student body. When you have made your choice install him to run the establishment the way I intended, but with you having a veto over any changes. In other words, Chris, the contracts that you and Mike negotiated to be the same for all staff now. At the beginning of each academic year thereafter, you and the new Chairman select the class leaders, both of you having full access to every student's history."

Chris was still feeling very poorly and asked Duncan for time to think about it.

"I guessed that would be your answer so I have drafted in a substitute history teacher on a short contract and appointed the Administrative manager temporary Chairman until you have decided your future."

Chris spent another week in recovery before going back to his parents. Duncan had a habit of getting what he wanted, and in the case of Chris, he almost courted him by paying for Jeff to be flown to Chris every weekend. That action sealed it for Chris. His recovery was much more rapid having his love with him every weekend, and by the end of the semester he called Duncan and said he would be prepared to go back to work on the terms previously discussed. There were no new students for this second semester of the year so Chris returned early and sat studying all the senior students' data. Using his own check list of attributes he wanted from the new Chairman, he eventually whittled it down until there was only one prominent candidate.

Darius Defoe was 20 years old. He was three years behind his peers because he had got entangled with a bad crowd at his last school when he was only fifteen. Before that time, he had been a first class academic and sportsman. Drugs and booze, absenteeism and lack of attention in class when he was there had ruined all that and at 18 he had left school with nothing. Duncan had got hold of him, had him locked down in rehab to dry him out and then offered him a place at the academy. In the year he had been there, he had returned his body to its previous peak of fitness and become an A+ student again. He was a class leader and his instructors' reports all indicate a natural leader.

Decision made and Chris was able to hit the gym every day to bring his own level of fitness back to what he had been before. The new semester started with Chris brimming with health. His first action before introducing the new regime to the students was to interview Darius.

Sat in the Chairman's office, Chris had Darius stand in front of his desk.

"Good morning Darius. The reason for this summons is that under Duncan's instructions I am to be temporary Chairman of the academy until I have selected a suitable replacement for his brother. You are the candidate, so I am going to start from the skin out to see if I think you can make the grade, physically and mentally. The first part is easy. I would like you strip naked for me, now, and get an erection."

Darius looked at Chris in shock, and then grinned. He disrobed with no obvious embarrassment, fisted himself to an erection and then took up a pose hands behind his back and a worried expression on his face.

Chris was almost instantly as hard as an iron bar. The young man was built, wide shoulders, incredible pecs, great legs, and in between them an 8 or 9 inch penis with an adequate ball sac beneath. He had a neat patch of light brown pubic hair and no other visible hair on his body apart from the same colour head hair cut in an old college boy style.

"Very nice Mr. Defoe. I expect to see a lot of you in the gym to keep that body as exciting as it is now."

Darius knew all about Chris and his sexual ability, so he smiled.

"Please redress and sit down."

Chris walked round his desk and sat in an armchair opposite Darius.

"I am going to give you the staff contract to read that Duncan and I agreed to several years ago. It gives the staff much more breathing space from student attention and worked well. All staff will be asked to sign it today when I meet with them after they are settled in. Students got good tutorials and good sex without overloading teachers. Teachers had enough free time to pursue their own interests and everybody was happy. Examination results were what was expected and almost all students went to Ivy League colleges. We are going to aim for that again. You can understudy me for a couple of weeks and then I will slide into the background and just be a teacher again taking over my classes from the temporary staff member. Before you institute any major change you must seek my approval, but other than that, you run the establishment the way you think is best for the students. Any questions?"

Darius was surprised, but pleased and his mind was working overtime.

"When I am Chairman, will I be able to start any meeting with you in the same way you started this one?"

Chris grinned.

"I can't think of anything in my contract that would preclude that action. Or any further action you wanted to take if you could justify it by bringing up any inadequacies you found in my performance, either as a teacher or as your mentor."

That was about as unequivocal as Chris could make it that he was ready and willing for more action with this very sexy man.

Darius was very definitely more than just a pretty body. He and Chris worked out together most days after instruction and used that period for their daily meetings. Within two weeks Chris considered he was good enough to take over as Chairman. He informed Duncan and then Darius.

"As of tomorrow morning, Darius, you can take over as Chairman. I will still be available any time to assist you, but I am going back to teaching. I will terminate my substitute's contract and see that he is paid the correct severance. I think Duncan has plans for you for next year if you make a success of your next two semesters, so don't let me down."

Darius was delighted and knew he was going to have fun with this well-buffed teacher who he knew had a reputation for being very raunchy in the right circumstances.

Chris had been in the habit of working out in a one piece suit, almost like a leotard, but with short sleeves and shorts. It buttoned all the way from the groin to the neck and made it unnecessary for him to wear a jock strap. The result was an incredibly erotic apparition. One day after their workout, Darius noticed that the gym was empty, so he addressed Chris.

"I think you were slacking in that workout Chris, and as you are supposed to set an example in every aspect of your work you need reminding that 100% effort is all that is acceptable. I think punishment should be given straight away to remind the wrongdoer, so strip, but be erect as your suit comes off."

This was the first time Darius had the opportunity to see this well-buffed teacher naked. Of course he had heard all the stories, but not studying history meant he had no classes with him.

The relationship between these two men had been very cordial since Darius took charge so Chris suspected that this was going to be a fun affair. He played with himself as he undid the fastenings. When he pulled the suit open to remove it from his shoulders his erect penis sprung clear. Darius was almost instantly fully erect. The body and groin looked totally edible. His dilemma now was that he was supposed to be rendering punishment which naturally would include being sucked by, and then fucking the teacher, but what he really wanted was to feel that gorgeous cock pulsing inside his own arse, after he had blown it for a while.

"Very nice Mr. Lovell. You may undress me now before I render punishment."

Chris had no problem with that. He had seen Darius naked and hard on his first day. Now that he had the opportunity to play with the body, he wasn't about to complain. Job done and the two men stood facing each other being quite open about scoping out each other.

"We always appear to be in competition Chris, so, I'm going to give you the chance to beat the system. Over to the wrestling mats and we'll 69. The first one to cum will provide the receptacle for the other one to get a good fuck."

Darius hoped he would cum first.

It really was no contest. Darius at 20 years old was almost certainly at the peak of his libido and Chris was a phenomenally experienced sex machine approaching 30 years old.

Both men loved it. Darius was so enthusiastic that he had no trouble swallowing Chris' balls, and licking and sucking on every inch of his cock. Chris was the same. Yes, they were both very sweaty, which under normal circumstances would have turned both men off the sex, but they were so horny for one another that they didn't worry about it. Chris took a monstrous amount of sperm as Darius exploded in his mouth. He pulled his cock away from Darius so that he wouldn't cum as well and looked at the grinning visage of his Chairman.

"I think we should retire to my apartment and shower before I take my pleasure from your love tunnel."

Darius could not have been happier with that suggestion because he was sure that would mean a long session instead of just a quick fuck. He wasn't wrong.

Chris wouldn't let Darius do anything once they were in his apartment. He took him to the shower and spent a long time pampering him. Chris loved it. Running his hands all over this gorgeous man was so erotic he almost orgasmed.

"Turn round, Darius, spread your legs wide. If I'm going to enter you I'm going to make sure you are uber clean."

Darius laughed, but the laugh quickly became a gasp as Chris first of all washed his arse thoroughly and then with soapy fingers slowly opened him up before rinsing out the hole and trying the taste test.

"Oh, fuck, Chris that feels so good."

Chris reached round the front and was amazed that Darius had an erection that was even harder than when he was being blown. The cock was hugging his belly and felt like a rod of iron.

"Mmm, I think you might be ready for me. Let's see what the bed feels like."

Chris was almost reaching overload looking at his Chairman lying on the bed, legs slightly spread, and arms behind his head, with that rigid cock hugging his tummy and ball sack with only a little slack left in it close up to the base of the cock. He spread the legs further and knelt between them so that he could lean in and use his tongue and lips to start driving Darius towards outer space. He slowly jacked the cock while he took the balls into his mouth, gripping them with his lips as he pulled them gently to get slacker. The precum was flowing so Chris used it on his thumb to run back and forth over the glans. Another very audible gasp from Darius was testament to his enjoyment of the action. Chris worked cock and balls hard, roving occasionally to the nipples. When he thought Darius might cum again, he left him alone while he spread the legs wider and then bent them up, holding them wide and well back. Chris told Darius to put a couple of pillows under his lower back. Job done and he had a pretty anus at just the right level to move in on it and lick hard from the upper end of the crack, across the anus to the perineum before licking behind the ball sac. Then it was stretching the anus more with Darius holding his legs back, before Chris started trying to tongue fuck him. That was too much, and Darius had another mighty orgasm.

"You weren't given permission to orgasm again. Now I shall have to punish you."

Chris started spanking Darius while he squeezed some lube onto his cock and took some more to lubricate Darius's love tunnel. He could feel that Darius was no virgin, so after ten, not very hard slaps, Chris entered him. He could feel how relaxed Darius was so he slid in all the way, putting pressure on the back of the thighs so that Darius's legs were almost touching the sides of his torso, then he started. A long slow fuck rotating his hips, then a few very fast entries, making Darius squeal. Chris also noted that his Chairman was sporting an erection again only minutes after his second orgasm of the evening. Being the consummate lover, Chris timed his orgasm to perfection, taking Darius with him for his third one.

Darius couldn't speak for ages. Chris slid out of him as he went soft and rolled over to lay beside him. Eventually Darius managed to gasp out.

"Now let that be a lesson to you. I expect total effort from you in future."

The two men turned their heads to look at each other and then burst into abandoned laughter.

"That was amazing, Chris. I'm normally a top, but I so wanted you to fuck me. Can we reverse rolls sometime, because I'd like to fuck you as well."

Chris leant in and placed a quite passionate kiss on Darius's lips before replying.

"I think I'd like that. How about tomorrow?"

Enthusiastic reply and then it was time for a clean-up and dress so that Chris could do his tutorials before dinner.

This regime was what Chris wanted. He loved the sex with all these well-buffed and intelligent young men and the ability to actually teach his subject. He told Jeff about his relationship with the Chairman and said that he hoped he would get another good one next year. Jeff wasn't worried. He knew that he had all of Chris's love now and he was having great sex away from Chris as well. Justin and Jake weren't greedy so the threesomes were fun. Weekends were mostly one on one with Chris, but occasionally there were raunchy foursomes.

These four young men could very easily have formed a very unusual family unit because of the love, and lust, that they shared with each other.

## Chapter 9

End of the school year brought another batch of first-class results for the senior class, and Duncan came home to start sorting colleges for them. In a meeting with Chris and Darius before they went off on vacation, Duncan dropped a bombshell on Darius.

"Before I start, Darius. You are under no obligation to accept this offer. Be aware that refusal will still see you into your first choice college if your results are good. I want you to stay on here for one more year as Chairman. You go to Princeton, but you take only half of your modules the first year to allow you a load of time here. I will pay you the full salary of a Chairman and keep Chris as your deputy for the time you are away at college."

Darius really wanted to go to M.I.T. so he told Duncan he would need to think about it. The result, a few days later was a call to Duncan from Darius' home.

"I'll accept your offer, Duncan, provided I can transfer to M.I.T. for my second year."

How he had worked it out was that he wouldn't lose a year if he took modules at Princeton that he would need at M.I.T. He could do two years' modules in one year here and then the same with modules at M.I T., thus completing all his first two years' modules in the correct time.

Duncan informed Chris, who was delighted. He was spending the holiday with Jeff, as normal now.

"We'll have to organise a threesome next semester, Jeff, so that you can sample my Chairman. You might even bump into him at college."

Jeff thought that would be interesting, and that was how it worked out.

~~~~

A new academic year with the now very acceptable system of class leader selection that Darius and Chris had used last year. Chris was satisfied with the choices when they completed the exercise. All of the new ones had shown leadership potential and dominance in their interviews. They had been shown a staff contract and knew the limits. One of them made the comment that even for minor punishment of a staff member he would send for Chris to witness. Darius showed his approval of that, as well as Chris.

The first few weeks passed and everything appeared to have settled down. Comments from other staff members gave Chris the impression that classroom action had been at a very acceptable level. All of them had been asked to strip by the class leaders, purely to show their authority, and that had been it. A new Spanish teacher had said nothing and Chris wondered about him because he was a new member of staff; very young, and extremely good looking. Chris thought the class leaders would have had a good look at, and feel of this boy to see what he was like with an erection.

It was a few days after that thought that Chris was paged at the end of a day's lessons. It was from one of the new class leaders asking him to attend Language 3 classroom. When he stepped through the door, the class leader who had been the one that impressed both him and Darius at interview was stood with the teacher at the front of the class. The teacher was Mario, the new Spanish teacher.

"Thanks for coming Chris. I know it isn't strictly necessary, but I want you to witness this staff punishment and understand the reason. Jose," pointing to a boy near the front, "was brought up in Madrid and is a fluent Spanish speaker. He is only here to get the grades, he doesn't need the instruction. He has picked up several mistakes in Mario's teaching today that I feel warrants some punishment and humiliation to make him more focused."

Chris looked round the class and asked.

"Do you all feel the same as your leader?"

Everyone nodded or voiced their assent.

"Very well Colin, go ahead then."

Colin turned to Mario who was already blushing.

"Two of the class are going to strip you, Mario. Follow their instructions to the letter or the punishment will be added to."

Colin left the teacher and stood by Chris.

Two boys moved to either side of Mario and started to unbutton his shirt before removing it. Then his belt was undone, the top of his trousers unclipped and the zip pulled down. They slid down revealing a pair of boxer briefs, nicely filled. The boys told the teacher to put his hands on top of his head. They dropped to their knees and under instruction had each foot raised in turn, and socks, shoes and trousers came off. Stood again and both students stroked front and back that area covered by the briefs until Mario started to grow. At a nod the boys lowered the briefs and removed them completely. A very presentable uncut cock was revealed, and quite a few boys—and Chris—were adjusting their own erections.

"Sit down, make yourself comfortable. I am going to play."

The student who said that dropped to his knees beside the chair, and with Mario's arms back behind his head, started to play with this young teacher. Chris had to admit he was gorgeous, and his cock and balls were something he would like to play with if he ever got the chance.

The cock wasn't completely erect and was already over 7 inches in Chris's estimation. The ball sac was perfect for playing with as well. The student played for a little while until Mario was as hard as iron. It looked gorgeous, the skin now only covering half of the glans. The student pulled it back completely and jacked it a few times before standing again.

"Now stand with your back to the class, let's see what we are going to be punishing."

Mario did as he was told and with his legs a little way apart showed a very nice rounded butt. The two students stroked it before telling him to kneel on the chair he had been sitting on, with his knees as far apart as possible and to lean over the back.

"Very pretty Mario, but if we have to do this again, we will shave all the hair from the area."

He nodded to his classmate and they moved in and pulled his cheeks apart so that everyone could see his anus. Then, using their spare hands they took turns thumb fucking him. It was so erotic that Chris noted several of the boys gasped as they orgasmed in their pants. A few minutes of that and they pulled out to administer five slaps each to the opposite cheeks, not too hard, but hard enough to leave a red glow. Stood facing the class again, looking very ashamed, Mario was addressed by the class leader.

"I doubt any punishment will be milder than that, Mario, so please make sure you only teach us what is correct in future. You may dress now, that is punishment complete."

Chris waited behind to talk to his fellow teacher.

"How are you feeling?"

Mario blushed.

"Very embarrassed. Unfortunately the boys were correct, so I have no complaint. I knew when I came here that the highest standards were required and I have read and accepted the terms of my contract. I just hope I don't mess up again because I have heard some of the more extreme punishments and giving blowjobs or being fucked by a student isn't high on my list of things to do."

Chris laughed then and patted his fellow on the back.

"You are a stunning hunk of male so I think you can guarantee that will happen sometime. The upside is that with that gorgeous cock, you will probably get some reciprocity in your tutorials."

Mario gave Chris a quizzical look.

"You sound like an enthusiast, Chris."

"I am, surely you've heard. I'm a complete cock hound. I give and take as often as I can."

That shook Mario and gave him food for thought. He thought Chris and the Chairman were incredibly attractive men when he saw them working out in the gym. He thought either or both of them taking advantage of him would be very pleasant.

Darius called on Chris after dinner that evening. Having heard about the staff punishment, he wanted to ask Chris his thoughts on the subject.

The knock on Chris' door was answered by Chris wearing just a pair of athletic shorts. It was quite obvious that they had no inner support and he was freeballing.

"Come in, Darius. Sit yourself down. Can I get you anything?"

Darius looked pointedly at Chris's groin and then looked at Chris, with a huge grin on his face.

"Mmm, a tube of lube and half an hour free use of your body."

Chris returned the grin, walked into his bedroom and came back with a tube of KY. Tossing it to Darius, and still grinning, he spoke.

"Be my guest."

"You slut. Does Jeff know how easy it is to play with you?"

"Oh yes, he knows I'm a slut as well, but he also knows I love him to pieces."

"Alright, chat first, then I'll take my half hour."

Chris got them both a glass of wine and then sat facing his Chairman.

"So, what are we going to chat about?"

"The new Spanish teacher. I understand you witnessed punishment on him today."

"Yes, it was a mild one so I didn't need to be there, but Colin insisted a member of staff be there as a witness. Mario gave some bad instruction, picked up by young Jose who is a native speaker of Castilian. The punishment was a strip, a little cock and arse play and then ten with bare hands. Nothing heavy, and talking to Mario afterwards, he admitted he deserved it and would be more careful in the future. The staff contract is working as it is supposed to as far as I'm concerned. I would like to be a fly on the wall at some of Mario's tutorials from now on though. My guess is that students are going to push the staff contract to the limit because our new boy is rather delicious naked and erect."

"I suppose you would like to try him as well?"

"God, yes, either passive or active would be fine."

"Damn, I didn't sit in on his interview so I never got the chance to strip him which is the normal interview system now."

Both men were laughing, but Chris still managed to speak through it.

"Well you're the Chairman, you can do virtually what you like. Call him for your own interview. You can use the excuse that you want to see how far he would let a student go before balking, and that would allow you to get a blowjob from his pretty lips and see how comfortable he is with a cock up his arse."

"You are a devious bastard, Chris Lovell, I am wondering if I should punish you now for being a slut."

The wicked look in Darius's eyes made Chris wonder if half an hour was going to be enough.

"Unless I want to leave I guess you can do what you like as my Chairman."

"Good, because I have decided to punish you, and tomorrow I want you to sit in on an interview with Mario."

Chris was almost panting at the thought.

"Now, stand up and drop your shorts."

Darius loved to look at this body. He saw it most evenings in the gym, but it still thrilled him, and the cock was to die for.

"Now undress me, and I want the best blowjob you have ever given. The number of strokes you get will depend on my rating of your ability."

This would be a labour of love for Chris. Darius had one of the most exciting bodies he had ever had sex with and his cock was gorgeous. Darius let Chris take him right to the edge before taking him through to his bedroom, and with him doggy fashion on his bed, Darius lubed them both and fucked Chris hard to a very quick orgasm. He fell across Chris' back and kept fucking him gently as he went soft and spoke in his ear.

"I am sure you are the most exciting fuck on the planet. I knew I wouldn't last very long."

He rolled off Chris who then dropped on to the bed as well alongside Darius.

"You are pretty special as well. Come back one evening when we have lots of time. I would love to finish what I started with my mouth, and then get you ready for a long fuck."

Two very contented men slept well that night.

~~~~

"Mario, the reason for this summons is because I need to be sure that the staff contract is never going to be a problem for you. You have already experienced a very mild punishment session. What I need to find out is how far one of those sessions could go before you balked against the action. I have asked Chris along as the staff representative to witness my actions. We are going to assume a serious failing on your part, with me as the class leader organising the punishment. Chris will act as another student that I will co-opt to up the humiliation."

Mario looked between the two and nodded his understanding.

"Now, disrobe for me—everything."

Mario hesitated for a few seconds and then shrugged and started undressing. Naked, he was as stunning as Chris remembered. Darius got out of his chair and walked round behind Mario. Close up, he wrapped his arms round the teacher and caressed his front. Starting by exciting the nipples he soon arrived at the groin and used his hands to play with the cock and balls at the same time. Chris was getting very excited and his erection was so hard it hurt. Darius started to slowly jack Mario's cock, drawing the skin fully back before covering the head again. At the same time he was cupping the balls and playing with them. He looked at Chris and realised he would probably cum in his pants in a few minutes. He let everything go and moved back to his seat.

"Very good, Mario. Now I think you should undress Chris. Let him get comfortable again and then give him a blowjob to orgasm, swallowing all his love juice."

Mario looked a little shocked but carried out the task. It was Darius' turn now to feel the need to orgasm. Watching Mario bobbing up and down on Chris's pole and playing with his balls was very erotic. When he had a mouthful of cum, he didn't look too upset, so Darius decided to go to the next level.

"With more practice you may be very good at that, Mario. In the meantime, you can undress me and I'm going to see if your other end is any good."

Mario spluttered a protest but Darius said nothing—he just stood clear of his desk and looked at Mario. Mario dropped his eyes and then undressed the Chairman.

"Now drape yourself over my desk, spread your legs wide and hold onto the other edge."

He looked at Chris, who was already erect again.

Darius was in heaven reaming out Mario with spit-slicked fingers. He even leant in and licked the anus a few times making sure Mario was getting very excited. Almost ready to cum, Darius had to pull off and take his time lubing Mario and himself. He moved in close, used his hands to stretch the cheeks more and placed his cock at the entry to Paradise.

"Relax now and push down."

Darius' look of anguish as he slid over the sphincter was seen by Chris who was sure he knew what was going to happen. Darius completed the entry, fucked Mario for probably less than a minute before having an almighty orgasm that nearly made him pass out.

"Oh God, Chris, you have to come here and try this."

Never slow for good sex, Chris lubed very quickly and slid into Mario as Darius withdrew. Having already cum once, Chris lasted a few minutes, but it was a struggle. Mario's insides were incredible and he was continually working his gluts. His orgasm was mind-bending and he slumped over Mario when he finished.

"If any of your students find out how incredible it is to fuck you, I imagine you will be having sex every day, during and after lessons. You are amazing."

Darius heard Chris' comment and when he stood up, he and Chris returned to their chairs. Mario stood in front of them blushing.

"We were both quite wicked taking things this far Mario, but I am glad we did. You are quite amazing. I think we owe you a reward for this. If you have two orgasms in you, you can take your pleasure with both of us."

"I think I would like that very much, but I would like it to be at a time and place of my choosing."

That was definitely not what Darius expected, so he spluttered a bit before agreeing. Chris laughed at that and replied to Darius' agreement.

"You may live to regret that decision Mr. Chairman."

Mario dressed and left.

Darius opened the new conversation.

"You are a great fuck Chris, but that man is shatteringly good. If he gives as good as he takes, I might end up volunteering to be his slave forever."

"Yes, me too. What worries me though is what he is planning as a time and place."

# Chapter 10

"Colin, will you and Jose remain behind after the lesson?"

Mario had thought about Chris and Darius and how they had combined to embarrass him and have complete sex with him. He had enjoyed it immensely. They were, after all, very sexy men, and their cocks had felt fantastic fucking him.

End of the lesson and the two students remained behind.

"Your punishment of me for a sloppy lesson was totally justified Colin, and your subsequent input, Jose, has improved the standard of this class and me personally. I have the opportunity to give you something of a reward, I think. For reasons you don't need to know, the Chairman and Mr. Lovell have given me carte blanche to use their bodies in a sex session. I wondered if you would both like to witness me fucking both of them."

Colin laughed, looked at a not so sure Jose, and replied.

"Would I ever, just tell me where and when?"

"The Chairman gets back from university early on Thursdays, and I have you for last lesson that day, so I thought I would get them here and we could indulge in this classroom. I will try to organise it that you both get involved, but I don't know how far I can push that one. Assistance, possibly, but no taking part would be my guess."

Jose was warming to this idea. He had noticed Chris frequently and heard the tales about him being a bit of a cock hound; and he had seen the Chairman working out in the gym and got a tingle thinking about seeing that bulge erect and bare.

Mario caught Chris in the staffroom and told him.

"I would like to take up the Chairman's offer on Thursday. After last lesson I would like you both in Languages 3. Please be cleaned internally and just wear sports clothes."

Chris thought this would be interesting, and so did Darius. When they walked into Languages 3, they were surprised to find two students there, still working with Mario.

"Ah, good afternoon, Sir, and Chris. The two students are Colin, who you both know, and my star student, Jose. I thought they might like to watch as a reward for the good work they have done so far this semester."

Before Darius or Chris could object, Mario continued.

"You didn't set any conditions, only that if I had two orgasms in me I could take them using your bodies. I did consider asking my whole class to remain behind to watch, but then decided Colin and Jose would be enough assistance for me."

Chris laughed, looked at Darius and spoke.

"I did warn you this might come back and bite you."

Darius shrugged.

"Very well, Mario. We are yours to command until you have orgasmed twice."

"Thank you, Chairman. Colin and Jose, would you like to take one each and undress them for me? I'm sure that in the process you can make sure they have erections by the time they are naked."

By the time Darius and Chris were naked there were five very hard cocks.

"Jose and Colin will obviously be uncomfortable with their penises so hard and restrained. Perhaps you two should undress them as well."

Chris and Darius weren't at all upset with the finished articles— both boys had very sexy appendages. Jose was quite thick and both were on the better side of average.

While the strip was going on, Mario had undressed as well.

"I will need to open up both of you before entering you, so to start—Chairman, would you get on my desk on your back? Chris, take one leg and Colin the other, and spread them wide, bend them up so that his knees are close to his shoulders. Use your other hand to spread his arse cheeks further so that I have free access. While I am preparing him, Jose, why don't you go to his head and let him blow you. I'm sure you would like to play as well, Chairman."

All positioned as Mario wanted and he pulled up a chair, sat comfortably he started fingering the chairman. With both hands free he could play with the cock and balls as well. Mario couldn't resist, the chairman's anus looked so inviting he leant in and rimmed him as well. Darius wasn't at all upset. He had a gorgeous thick cock in his mouth and a pair of hands and a tongue playing havoc with his senses in his lower regions. When Mario was about ready to cum, he stopped all action and stood up to watch Jose while he calmed down a little. Then he lubed his cock and the Chairman's anus before positioning for entry. He stroked the backs of Darius's thighs as he applied pressure and slid gently over a very relaxed sphincter. An incredibly sensuous slow fuck followed, with Mario playing with the chairman's cock and balls. The resulting orgasms were fantastic. Darius' torso was smothered in what looked like a gallon of cum; there was so much of it. Jose was so turned on by all the action that he soon after filled Darius' mouth with his own orgasm.

"That was quite excellent, Chairman. Would you join me for a clean-up so that Chris can get me ready to fuck him? Chris, perhaps you should get some practice exciting Colin while we are away."

There was a ripple of laughter there because it was quite obvious that Colin was within an ace of having his own orgasm just from watching the action.

Sat in his chair, all cleaned up, Mario enjoyed the attention that Chris lavished on his cock. Chris wasn't complaining either; Mario had a gorgeous appendage. Time to move on, he carried out the same action on Chris that he had done to Darius, allowing Colin to orgasm in Chris's mouth while receiving a very erotic fuck from his colleague. Darius and Jose were the only two hard cocks after Mario had cum, so he suggested to the chairman that quite voluntarily he and Jose could satisfy each other. A damp squib finish unfortunately. Both men were so turned on that they only jacked each other for a couple of minutes before both had orgasms.

All cleaned up and dressed, Darius concluded the event.

"Thank you gentlemen, that was very stimulating."

Everybody went their separate ways with broad grins spread across their faces.

# Epilogue

Life didn't change very much for Chris after the session with Mario. He still had as much sex as he wanted and still produced interesting and well-presented lessons. Classroom punishment for him was a non-existent event, but his tutorials made up for it.

Jeff came most weekends, even when Chris was refereeing soccer matches.

Justin and Jake were frequent visitors as well with the consequent foursomes.

The college years flew by, and after graduation, Justin and Jake went to work for Justin's father. Jeff wanted to be near Chris and went to work on Wall Street. They bought a house between their places of work, and Duncan sanctioned Chris living off campus. The result was a huge decrease in the amount of sex he had with students, but that was more than made up for by being with Jeff every night.

The academy evolved and became more mainstream in the way the staff were treated. Duncan still insisted on highly qualified teachers, and they were still punished if their standards slid, but the sexual content of those punishments was toned down.

The structure of the hierarchy changed as well. Chris became the director of the academy and ran it with the class leaders as before. The emphasis on these appointments now though was leadership. Results continued to improve and an old boys' association was formed with an annual reunion on the calendar. For years that was an excuse for Chris and Jeff, Justin and Jake to renew their sexual liaisons.

## ~~The End~~

## WANT FREE COPIES OF MY BOOKS?
Just visit my blog and download free copies of my books:
http://dexter-chase.awesomeauthors.org/dexter-chase/

Here is a sample from another story you may enjoy:

# OWNED
## *in* SINGAPORE

GAY SUBMISSION EROTICA

# DEXTER CHASE

"Alex, come in, sit down. Coffee?"

Alexander Dupree did as he was told and thanked his boss. "Black with two, please, Sir."

He was very wary as to why he was being talked to in such a friendly manner. His performance to date had earned him two warning letters. The next time it would be dismissal, and the last thing Alex could afford at the present time was the sack.

"I'm sure you are aware that your performance this year has been well below what we have come to expect from you. Two years ago you were on track to make partner. Then, a little less than a year ago it all started to unravel for you. We have been very disappointed because we saw you as the future. You were our senior associate, and the youngest. I have talked to the other partners and we have made a decision concerning your future."

Alex took the coffee offered to him as his boss spoke. Was this the big push being built up to by giving him all the reasons for it? He knew he had been underperforming. During his first two years with the partnership he had closed so many difficult deals he had become something of a legend. He was only 26, single and considered a premium catch for any female. His apartment in the centre of town was furnished in the height of good taste and luxury, his BMW convertible was less than two years old. His level of debt was frightening.

The boss sat back down behind his desk and looked hard at his fallen star.

"I am sure you are aware that our best efforts to secure the deal with Straits Technical have not borne fruit. We think that in your hay day you would have tied this up with little effort so we are giving you a last chance to prove yourself. We are sending you to Singapore to replace Jason Oakley on the negotiating team. He will remain to assist you, but this will be your deal to make or lose. If you bring the deal back we will tear up your two written warnings, re-instate you as senior associate and guarantee you a partnership in twelve months if you then continue to perform the way you did before the drop in standards."

Alex knew he could do it if he could just get over his feeling of loss at his poor performance. He had no idea why he had lost it, but after the first written warning he got depressed and his underperformance accelerated. If he could start again he knew he would be ok. The pressure to succeed where everyone else had failed just acted as a challenge to him now.

"Thank you, Sir. I won't let you down."

"We hope not, Alex. We don't want to lose you but we need results to be better than your last year has produced."

Coffee finished, detailed folder presented to him.

"Take that away and absorb it. Be ready to leave for Singapore after the weekend."

That was it. Alex spent the weekend absorbing the contents of the folder. He spoke to Jason Oakley for hours getting all the personal details of the negotiating team from Singapore Technical. It was his ability to get the opposing negotiating teams onside that had been his greatest asset, now he needed it again, big time.

Monday morning, a first class seat on Singapore Airways and he was on his way. He was so pleased he could link his laptop to a power source because virtually the whole of the flight he was working on it. Jason met him at Changi and whisked him away to his hotel.

"We are going in for another round of talks after lunch, Alex. Do you want to sit in or have a rest and start fresh tomorrow?"

"I'll sit in, Jason. Introduce me to the other team and I'll just observe today. Conference with our team tonight and then I'll take over tomorrow morning."

Jason had mixed feelings being replaced by this much younger man who he knew had failed to shine the last twelve months.

"Very well, Alex. I'll give you all the support I can, but believe me, you will need a miracle to get Phillip Chen to go down our road in this deal."

"But he is only one man, what about the others?"

"The others are lackeys. They just say what Phillip tells them to. If you crack him you have the deal, but none of us have been able to."

During the afternoon sitting, Alex observed Phillip Chen closely, not missed by Phillip himself. Phillip had noticed Alex for different reasons to what should have been expected.

By the time Alex went to bed that night, despite the 8 hour time zone change, he slept like a baby, completely wiped out, but confident he had a handle on this whole deal, ready to do battle.

If you enjoyed this sample then look for **Owned In Singapore**.

**Also by this Author:**

Mastered

Go For Goal Or... Guy?

Ruin

The Loser

Forced by the Military

Lucifer's Academy

So Full It Hurts!

Bully to Slave

Play & Pretend

The Submissive Bad Boy

Unexpected Island Mates

No Hoper

Chance of the Heart

Boy Beauty Contest

Finding Michael

Caribbean Fun

Bareback On Board

Weird Arrangement

Love on the High Seas

Lovely Boy

# Owned in Singapore

\*\*\*

## *I REALLY LOVE Reviews!*

If you enjoyed this book, please share the love and don't forget to leave a review on Amazon or the site of any other retailer you purchased this book from!

I highly appreciate your reviews, and it only takes a minute to write & post one. I can't tell you how much this means to me!

You'll find the list of all my books on my Author Central page... just in case you'd like to leave a review for other books of mine you've read but didn't have time to leave a review.

\*Amazon Author Central – http://www.amazon.com/Dexter-Chase/e/B00PDYM4FM

One Last Thing, For Kindle Readers...

When you turn the page, Kindle will give you the opportunity to rate this book and share your thoughts on Facebook and Twitter. If you enjoyed my writings, would you please take a few seconds to let your friends know about it? Because... when they enjoy they will be grateful to you and so will I.

Thank You!

**Dexter Chase**
dexter_chase@awesomeauthors.org

## About the Author

**Dexter Chase** is a writer of hot, gay erotica stories in both paperback and Kindle versions.

His very first book published is <u>Mastered (Sensual Tales from Ancient Egypt)</u> which is about an eighteen-year old Ajax, who was taken as a slave and brought to a great house by a high-ranking soldier.

Check out his books and you'll enjoy extreme gay erotica of all time.

**You may also like the books by these authors:**

# Wayside

# GL😊RY H😊LE

## MM First Time Gay Romance

## DICK PARKER

I looked at the guy. He was in his late thirties or maybe forty. He was decent looking. He looked clean and pretty normal, like a businessman or some kind of worker. He walked to the toilet and went inside.

I waited ten minutes to be sure he wasn't just a regular guy who went in to shit. He was still in there so I walked over to the toilet. I moved my bike so he knew someone was out there and then I went inside. I could see his feet under the stall next to the urinals. I walked up to the closest urinal to the stall.

I could see him in the hole in the wall. He was watching. Damn, I was so nervous my hands were shaking. I stepped up to the urinal and pulled the front of my shorts down. I was hard and my dick was wet on the tip from pre-cum. I stood there and stroked it a little. Then I turned a bit so he could see it.

"Nice."

Oh shit. I was so nervous I thought I was going to puke.

"Are you horny?"

"Yeah," I whispered.

"You've got a nice dick. Ever get it sucked?"

"Uh uh."

"Would you like to?"

"Yeah kinda."

"You sound young. Are you eighteen?"

"Yeah, just turned a month ago."

"Oh yum. I love young cocks. Put it over here."

I looked down and I could see his mouth. He opened it and stuck his tongue out.

I moved closer and put my dick down by the hole. He licked the tip with his tongue. I jumped.

"Calm down. I'm not going to hurt you, kid."

"I'm pretty nervous."

"Is this your first time?"

"Yeah."

"Put it in the hole."

Oh man. It was now or never. But wait, what if he was some kind of a madman and had a big knife and cut my dick off? Or what if he bit down on it and bit the head off? That was crazy. What was wrong with me? I had a guy with his mouth open who wanted to suck my dick.

I put it in the hole. He put it in his mouth immediately. His mouth was warm and wet and his tongue licked around the head of my dick and the underside of it. Oh man it felt so good and then the tickle started. I was cumming!

"Oh fuck mister, I'm cumming!"

He jumped a bit when the first squirt shot out. Then he sucked and licked and milked my dick until I had to hold onto the top of the stall or I'd have fallen down. My dick was limp and red when I pulled it out of the hole.

"Damn kid that was a hell of a cum. You must have been saving up."

"Sorry, I was so excited I couldn't stop it."

"No problem. How did you like it?"

"It was great. It was short but nice."

"I'll be here next Thursday at the same time," he said.

"I'll see you then, mister."

I pulled the front of my shorts up. My dick felt warm and nice as it nestled down by my balls. I got my bike and started back toward town. Then I realized, I'd told my family I was camping. Shit, I had to find someplace to sleep.

By the time I got to town it was thundering in the west. It was going to rain so I had a good reason to go home. I pulled into the yard just as it started raining. My brother asked me if I caught any fish and I said no. Then I went in my room and undressed and went to the bathroom to shower. I stood in front of the mirror and looked at myself. My dick was still kind of red and it looked pretty nice. It hung down over my balls and was pretty thick and about four inches long when it was soft. Hard, it was six inches.

My pubic hair was light brown like the hair on my head and it was thick but my bush wasn't very wide. I'd seen some of the guys at school who had huge bushes. Mine was just a couple inch wide strip of hair across the top of my dick. I turned so I could see my ass and it looked nice too. I tried to see my butt hole but couldn't do it. I wondered what it looked like. I lifted my arms and looked at my armpit hair. I'd waited forever for a hair in there. Many of my friends had pit hair and it took me forever to get some. But now that I got some, it had come in pretty thick.

My blue eyes were the best feature of my face. They looked really nice, looking back at me. I smiled and thought I looked pretty cute. I knew what a cute boy looked like and I think I fit the bill. That kid at the wayside must have thought I was cute or he probably wouldn't have showed me his cock. Damn that was something.

"I wonder how many other guys are out there who like guys like I do?" I thought. "I wish I'd find someone my age in town so I didn't have to go to the wayside."

I got in the shower and washed. When I washed my dick and balls I boned up. My dick was ready again for a good cum. My brother was in bed when I went back to the room. He was reading and had headphones on.

"Have fun tonight?" he asked.

"Oh hell yeah. It was fun."

Johnny was sleeping and I lay there with a hard on. Damn that guy's mouth felt nice on my cock. I wish it had taken longer. I wondered what else guys would do with me if I met them there? I knew I was going back soon.

Friday Mom and Dad were at work and Johnny had a baseball game. I wanted to go to the wayside again. I showered and dressed in some cut off jeans that I'd cut pretty short. I had to be careful or my balls would show in the leg hole. I put on a white tight tank top and flip-flops and jumped on my bike.

When I pulled into the wayside there was a car parked but I didn't see anyone around. I parked my bike by a picnic table and sat on the table waiting to see what happened. A minute later an old guy came out of the toilet and went to his car. He started it and drove away. Well shit, no blowjob there.

I waited. A while later a car pulled in with a woman in it with two little kids. They went to the toilet and left. I was getting pretty discouraged. I went in the toilet and looked at the messages on the wall. There were a lot of them and I hoped one said something about Friday but none did. I was just about to go back to my picnic table when I heard a car drive up. Shit, now what?

I stood there for a second and then went in the stall. I pulled my shorts down and sat on the toilet. I heard footsteps coming up the sidewalk and the door opened. I saw sneakers and jeans below the stall wall. The guy walked up to the urinal and I heard him unzip.

I was holding my breath. I leaned down and looked through the hole. He was standing close to the urinal and I could hear him pissing. Shit he wasn't looking for sex.

I watched just in case I could get a look at his cock. He stopped pissing and I could tell he was shaking his cock off. He shook it and shook it. It seemed like he shook it way more than he needed to. Then I could see his hand and it was making a stroking motion. Holy shit, he was looking!

I didn't know what to do. My dick got hard and I took hold of it and stroked it while I peeked through the hole. After a minute he stepped back and I could see his dick. It was hard and it was about the same size as mine. He turned toward the hole.

"How's it going?" he asked.

"Okay."

He turned away.

"How are you?" I asked.

"I'm good. How old are you?"

"I'm eighteen."

"You sound younger."

"I promise I'm eighteen."

"What you looking for?"

"I'm not sure. I'm new to this."

He turned back and put his cock close to the hole.

"Do you suck cock?"

"I um, I never have. I came here last night and a guy sucked mine. So I came back today."

"You want to try it?"

"Wow, I'm not sure."

"No problem. You want me to suck you off?"

"Really? You'd do that?"

"I'd be a fool to turn down an eighteen-year-old kid."

"Okay, so what do we do?"

"Open the door."

I unlatched the stall door. It opened and there stood a guy who looked like he was in his mid-twenties. He was wearing jeans and a sleeveless tee shirt. He was very nice looking and had a fantastic body. His dick was sticking out of his pants.

He stepped in and shut the door.

"If someone else comes in, you lift your feet up so they only see one pair of feet," he said.

"Cool."

His dick was six inches from my face. He saw me looking at it.

"You want to touch it?"

I nodded…

If you enjoyed this sample then look for <u>Wayside Glory Hole</u>.

# Prisoner of His Heart

Hot Gay Romance

Chris Johns

I remember Toy being so proud that the King was the longest ruling monarch in the world, longer even than our Queen Elizabeth. We went to Pattya for some beach time and the wonderful fun filled gay area. We stayed in the Nippa Lodge, right on the beach. We played badminton, swam in the pool and the sea, and I sunbathed. Toy didn't; to him a dark skin meant "peasant," that is... someone who worked outdoors. He couldn't be confused with them, so he stayed under a beach umbrella and read; he was always reading. No doubt that was the reason he was so good at his course subjects. He never ceased to please me with his enthusiastic approach to life, always appearing to be happy, and I very quickly fell in love with him.

Both of us were almost virgins in sexual experience; we had both played around at school, but just normal boy/boy experimentation, so our lovemaking became a voyage of discovery for both of us. It was ages before we got beyond the basics of mutual hand jobs, and blowjobs were magical when they happened. The big one was a long time in coming... Toy was so small, and I was worried about hurting him. Eventually, he wanted it more than me so we tried it. The result was a bucket of tears from him, and a vow that he would be mine forever, now that I had taken his virginity. I'm sure every first timer says something similar so I didn't set much store by the words.

During my time in prison, I just hoped that he would find another lover to look after him in our big bad world. I determined as we drove towards Cambridge that I would use my time before college started to find out what happened to him. I had contact details for his sister, so if they hadn't changed I should be able to find out what I wanted to know.

I held my breath as the locksmith gained entry for me and stood back. I opened the door, and the first thing that struck me was the smell. It took me back to my childhood... days spent in the country roaming in the woods and fields on camping trips. It smelt of summer, lilacs, and freshly mown grass. I turned to my foreign office escort with a bemused look on my face.

He had picked up on it as well, having been informed that he might well have to take me to a hotel to start with. He just shrugged. From the entrance hall I walked into the lounge; it was neat and tidy, clean as a whistle, with fresh flowers on display, and looking round the walls I could see landscape posters of Thailand, all neatly framed. The remainder of the flat was the same…immaculate. The bedroom told me what my mind was finding hard to accept. On the bedside table was a picture of Toy and me taken at the Royal Palace in Bangkok the Easter of my visit, and on the other side a picture of his parents and sister. I sat down with a bump. Toy was still in residence, but how?

I recovered my composure and told my escort I would be fine. Not to worry about keys…I had the feeling they would appear sometime today; if not, I would telephone for the locksmith to return with a new lock. When they had gone, I rummaged around to see what else there was. The wardrobe and chest of drawers in the master bedroom were as before…all my clothes neatly hung and stored, all smelling fresh. They would, of course, be too big for me until I put my weight back, but that was going to save me a load of money replacing what I thought had been lost. The kitchen cupboards were full of Thai herbs and spices, lots of fresh food in the refrigerator and I noted a total lack of alcohol. Good boy…he hadn't changed. I sat back in the lounge and pondered why he was still here, four years, so he was twenty now to my twenty-three. He should have finished his course so why was he still in England?

It was late afternoon when I heard a key in the lock. I stood up and waited. He appeared in the doorway and saw me. I thought he was going to faint he looked so shocked. Neither of us moved for what seemed like an eternity before he suddenly burst into tears and fell to his knees.

"I'm sorry, I'm so sorry, please forgive me."


If you enjoyed this sample then look for **Prisoner Of His Heart**.

# DONNY MUMFORD

# OLIVER'S
# ADVENTURES
## A SEQUEL OF OLIVER'S WILDWOOD VACATION

This summer I worked, fell in and out of love, and had the time of my life vacationing at Wildwood New Jersey. Playtime is over now, though; tomorrow, I'm off to college. It's my freshman year at the University of Pennsylvania. All the preparations have been done and I'm nervously ready to go first thing in the morning. After a good night's sleep, we start out very early in the morning, like five o'clock, to be accurate. It's a five-hour drive for me in my Mini Cooper convertible. The car was a graduation present from my rich, albeit, mixed-up brother, Christian. I get to drive my car, and my parents insist on going with me, but in their SUV. Actually, me driving to college is a major deal and initially, I didn't think I'd be allowed. Freshmen living in dorms aren't normally permitted to have a car on campus. I side-stepped that technicality by applying for an "Assistance-Group" exception. I was accepted and got a sticker to park my car on campus. The Assistance Group is a very old campus organization with the mission of providing free assistance to incoming freshman. I'm now a member of this do-gooder group and it seems an easy way to get two credits each year, but mainly, I just wanted a parking pass for my car.

The Assistance Group members are asked to help another freshman in any number of ways. Maybe I'll be an aide to someone who needs help getting around, a student on crutches perhaps or a blind student, God forbid. Or maybe I'll have to chauffeur someone to a doctor's appointment or, hell, I don't know. If a student needs assistance, I'm their boy. I don't know that much about it because I didn't read all the materials they sent me. I also have no idea why I was admitted to the group, not that I really care. I've never been much of a joiner, but I really needed to have my car with me. How else would I get to see friends back home? So, no problem, dude, sign my ass up for whatever. The University of Pennsylvania is inside the city limits of Philadelphia so there aren't any rolling hills or expansive lawns on campus. There's a lot of cement and black-top and a lot of brick and ivy-covered old buildings. It's all new to me: the energy and excitement of big city life, plus the atmosphere of a major Ivy League university all wrapped together, wow! I liked everything about it when exploring the campus during my high school's senior class trip last May.

After arriving on campus, I need to wait forty-five minutes for my dad and mom to arrive. Dad drives agonizingly slow. Pretending I recently arrived myself, I tell dad, "I haven't had time to scope out the reception and admissions area, but I believe it's down this street." Mom smiles proudly, but my Dad makes a face like he know I'm full of it, and of course I am. I had plenty of time to drive around and find out where we should go. Registering turns out to be an extremely tedious experience, that's the best thing I can say about it. We won't be starting classes for two days, but there are orientation meetings that freshman should attend. That still leaves a lot of free time for me to get reacquainted with the campus. As part of registration, I'm assigned my dormitory building and my room, so off we go to have a look at my room and unpack the cars. When we get there, I'm pleased with both the dorm I'm in and the room. I immediately think about Cristobal, who I met during my class trip and with whom I had my very first sexual experience with. A very pleasant and exciting one it was too. I was in his dorm and right off it's apparent how much better my dormitory is than his. Better because my dormitory is centrally located near all the main classroom areas, dining rooms, recreation facilities, etc. But, by far, the number one reason my dorm is better is because there's a private bathroom for each of the rooms on the first floor. And, my room's on the first floor. No waiting for elevators, but much more importantly, no community bathing and shitting and such. On the wall next to the front door, a three-by-five card has been taped. On it, written in big block letters, "NICKERSON/GALLO".

If you enjoyed this sample then look for **Oliver's Adventures**.

# Our First Meeting

## The Notebook

D.D. WATSON

He searched for shelter having no clue where to turn. Exposed to the world and vulnerable, skin damp and sprinkled with dirt from running through the woods.

The forest was dense and had no visible trails; the sun was going down and the entwined branches blocked out what little light he had. Tears welled in his eyes, but he fought them back refusing to show any form of weakness.

He found shelter in a cave that was for now, his only refuge; he fled from his captors or maybe; they let him escape? He wrapped his arms around his shivering body as he kneeled down to the ground exhausted from the run he had to endure on barefoot. His body screamed from the torments; only moments ago inflicted on him…

***

Arian Taylor-Kinney, nicknamed Rin by his fathers, scribbled hastily in his notebook the story that burned in his head. A college student with brilliant soft golden-brown eyes, long auburn hair that shaped his soft face and seemed to obey as it drifts across his magnet eyes when he read or smiled with his curvy lips. His trim built helped draped his clothing that usually was just tee shirts and jeans. Arian hasn't had experience in relationships, sexual or monogamy. He was homeschooled by his father from pre-school to the last day of high school.

When entering college he wasn't as overwhelmed with his academics as he and his parents predicted, socializing was a bit different, but not problematic he has been to different groups where he'd made friends growing up, dance, soccer, swimming, and theater.

During his first semester he mostly focused on finding his classes, having to share his views in front of strangers, appointments, lectures, and due dates.

He bypassed moving into the dorms something his fathers disapproved. Arian reasoned that they lived close to the campus and that he would make friends just as easy commuting back and forward and that it would just be a waste of money.

As he settled into his second semester, he began to notice other people who were interested in him, males and females. Arian didn't want to be distracted from his studies, so he made friendships but nothing more. To tame the growing urges he had from the offers he was receiving from his classmates, mainly the males, he continued a method he performed back in high school to write his desires down in spiral notebooks.

The fantasies detail in location, positions; the men involved and the level of heat they were performing. Arian spilled his darkest, purest desires out on the line paper and what started with one notebook turned into more. He even came across a muse that seemed unreal, but he did become Arian's star player in most of his fantasies.

Sitting outside was a joy for him because during his younger days, and on nice weather his father performed a few of his lessons at the park or in their backyard. On this one particular day, Arian enjoyed relaxing alone on a bench under the shade of trees while writing and watching passersby.

"Hey Arian," said a tall blonde male who sat beside him as if he was a close friend. His physique was impressive showing through his close-fitting tank top and shorts as he put his arm behind Arian's shoulders resting it on the bench. Staring at the brawny arm, Arian wondered if he could dodge it—if his interloper decides to embrace him.

"Sorry, do I know you?" he asked leaning forward closing his notebook and grasping it firmly in his lap.

"Sure you do— Peter we have the same English class, Professor Law?" he smiled a familiar smile that Arian's become accustomed to. The same grin that said more behind it than it presented. His hand dropped to Arian's upper back, he tensed up and tried to shift away.

"I'm sorry I'm pretty sure I would remember you." Peter leaned closer placing his free palm on top of Arian's whom gripped his notebook even tighter.

"Well to be honest you always had your head in a book or writing something in that notebook but I did make it my business to sit nearby you and ask for a pencil."

"That was you?"

"Yes and it hurts my feelings that you don't remember me."

"Sorry, Professor Law had a lot of notes to take down, and he had asked me to use my notes as a class reference," Arian lied.

"Well, you can make it up to me." His fingers slid down Arian's spin sending heated tension throughout his skin.

"I can?" Arian shifted again and managed stop the message the sensation was sending to his cock.

"Dinner at my place," said Peter, who ignored Arian's evading.

"Your place?"

"Yeah, I have an apartment, my parents' ideal to help me study," he said looking Arian over intently as he moved his fingers from his back to reach around and touch his face.

"Is it helping?" Arian asked turning his face to avoid Peter's touch on his cheek only to get caught locking eyes with his green orbs. Peter managed to catch Arian's chin and hold his gaze.

"Well, why don't you come over with your notes and you can test me?"

"Well I—"

Just before Arian was about to turn him down a male student ran up to them grabbing Peter's arm.

"Peter you need to come quick."

"Not now Sam, I'm busy," he snapped keeping his attention on Arian.

"But your car." That did it; Peter leaped from the bench and fixated his full concentration on Sam.

"What about my car?"

"All the tires are missing."

"What?!"

"Also the engine."

"Are you kidding me?"

"Go see for yourself."

Peter darting away, Sam remained behind as Peter raced off and turned to Arian, who was standing collecting his things to head to class.

"Where you headed?" asked Sam. Arian looked at him with a puzzled look.

"To class."

"Aren't you concerned about Peter's car?"

"It's none of my business."

"That's not what I saw a moment ago you two looked quite comfy."

Arian wasn't skilled in relationships but did know when someone was jealous.

"Look, I scarcely knew Peter until now so whatever—this is," he gestured with his hand. "He's all yours."

"Damn right he is. I see what you do to men," he snapped, stomping off.

"What did he mean by that?" thought Arian, as he walked to his next class.

A young male watched the scene with full concentration as if he was watching a play. He held a can of unopened soda between his ring-covered fingers. As Arian walked away, Sam approached him.

"All better?" he asked taking the soda from him.

"Yeah thanks, I owe you."

"So you'll cover for me at work on Saturday?"

"Can do."

"Thanks Cross you're a life saver," he said popping the cap and taking a deep swallow.

"No, you are," replied Cross, gathering his messenger bag that strangely resembled Arian's that Sam noticed.

"Hey, I know it's none of my business but if you like him then just tell him."

"I couldn't handle the rejection."

"Cross you're beautiful, if you weren't so into him I'd ask you out."

"But I am into him and—I would like to handle it in my way."


If you enjoyed this sample then look for **Our First Meeting**.

# Here Comes Trouble

BECOMING GAY EROTICA

ANGUS MacGREGOR

Sitting on this ridge top, I wonder why in the hell I ever agreed to come on this elk hunt. I don't really even like hunting. I used to, but not so much anymore. I mean, I love the camaraderie, and being outside in Oregon, and the beer. I love the beer the most. The whiskey is pretty great as well. I love the way the mist and clouds hug the mountains of the coast range like an old lady wearing a fur. The carpet of endless green, an ocean of Douglas fir that slides down the hills and tucks in and around rock outcroppings and pulls up its skirts for the rivers to splash through. The smell of wood smoke and the crisp autumn air that is just waiting to turn blue and bathe the mountains in frigid winter. But something is up with this hunting trip. It has been strange since the minute we got on the road. What am I saying? It's been weird for months.

Now that I am paying attention, and if I am honest, it's been going on since Emma and I met back in college. I dreaded the whole – "meet the parents" thing. I'm a real outgoing guy, not shy in the least. I don't have any confidence issues either. I mean, I'm lucky enough to have good looks and the kind of personality that most people seem comfortable with. But it's different meeting the parents. There's a whole other level of scrutiny and judgment that be part of that.

But I should back up, because this story began months before that, shit, it was years. I was the baby of my family, Chad Alonzo Martinez. A big brown-eyed, black haired, tanned little ball of energy. I had a brother that was ten years older than me. I adored him, but he and I had zero in common and hardly spent any time together at all. I was barely in grade school when he was graduating from high school. I did get to spend about a year in his bedroom before he moved out. See, I had a sister too, and she and I had shared a bedroom for quite a while, but as she got older, she was done with having a younger brother in the middle of her business. Jack said he didn't mind, which looking back, I find hard to believe. He was practically a grown man and I was just this cute little boy. But back then, I went to bed so early, he was rarely in the room with me. He came to bed way after me and I was always up and out of the room before he starts stirring since he didn't have a first period class.

There were a few nights I woke up in the middle of the night to look over and see him stroking his cock fast and furious. I knew better than to interrupt something so obviously private. But I would lay still and watch in fascination as his hand moved silently up and down his huge penis. His eyes would close and he would fondle his balls, belly, and nipples as he jacked. A few times, I even saw him seemingly slide a finger up his ass, which was both mystifying and utterly shocking at the same time. In the end, he would raise his furry ass off the mattress and send a fat rope of semen blasting up on his hairy chest and belly. He would usually grab some scandalously grimy cum rag from underneath the bed and wipe off his chest and then turn over and begin to snore. I had no idea what the whole thing meant, but it was fascinating nonetheless. A few years later, I followed in his footsteps and began rubbing one off every night before sleeping, secretly thinking my older brother for the lesson he didn't even know he was providing.

There were a few conversations that also contributed to my sexual education. Jack tended to take really long showers, probably because he was masturbating the whole time in there as well. Very often, I would be brushing my teeth or taking a little boy dump when he would open up the curtain and step out of the shower in all his muscled, hairy glory. Most often, his penis would be still erect and I would watch astonished as it bobbed and bounced on top of impossibly huge testicles. Several times he caught me watching and made a point to walk over and rub my face in his crotch, playfully, but all the same, shocking for a little kid. Sometimes he would reach down and grab my penis or nuts and give them a playful squeeze and say, something ridiculous.

"Damn, little bro, your dick is almost as big as mine. You are gonna be hung like a horse by the time you are in high school."

If you enjoyed this sample then look for **Here Comes Trouble.**

# WANT FREE COPIES OF MY BOOKS?

Just visit my blog and download free copies of my books:
http://dexter-chase.awesomeauthors.org/dexter-chase/

www.ingramcontent.com/pod-product-compliance
Lightning Source LLC
Chambersburg PA
CBHW071357170626
46811CB00003B/1158